Congratulations on obtaining this book. It is shockingly brilliant. If, however, it is the first Nanny Piggins book you've read (perhaps because you're a numerologist who pathologically avoids anything involving the numbers one through seven) or if you have read the first seven books but you can't remember a thing about them because you read so much pig-based literature that it is all a blur, either way – do not fret.

You will easily pick it all up as you go along. Each Nanny Piggins book is a stand-alone story. In fact, each chapter is a stand-alone story. So feel free to tear your book up into the ten separate chapters and share them with nine friends, or nine enemies. (This book is so good it may turn an enemy into a friend.)

But if you are an anxious type who wants to be fully prepared for what lies ahead, here are a few pointers to get you started.

Nanny Piggins is the world's greatest flying pig. (She doesn't have wings; she gets blasted out of cannons. Or, rather, she used to get blasted out of cannons before she ran away from the circus due to the lack of chocolate biscuits in the employee break room.)

She became a nanny when she saw a sign on the Green's front lawn, and as it was raining and she did not have an umbrella, she applied immediately.

Mr Green, her employer, is a dreadful man. He is a tax lawyer. No more need be said. If you imagine a tax lawyer you will have a pretty good idea of everything you need to know about him. But in defiance of genetics his three children, Derrick, Samantha and Michael, are a delight. Nanny Piggins' brother, Boris the ballet-dancing bear, also lives with them (although Mr Green doesn't know this, because he is too unobservant to notice the ten-foot-tall, highly emotional Russian bear living in his garden shed).

There are lots of other wonderful characters, including a very kind Police Sergeant, a hygiene-obsessed rival nanny, a petty school principal, a retired Army Colonel with romantic aspirations, several very exotic former circus colleagues and thirteen beautiful, glamorous and often evil identical twin sisters, just to name a few. But I won't describe them all in detail, because it will be nice for you to have some lovely surprises as you read along.

So find yourself a comfortable chair and a nice big chocolate bar, then sit back and enjoy this book.

Yours sincerely,

R. A. Spratt, the author

# Nanny Piggins

## AND THE RACE TO POWER

BOOK 8

## R. A. SPRATT

RANDOM HOUSE AUSTRALIA

*To Peregrine & Eva*

A Random House book
Published by Random House Australia Pty Ltd
Level 3, 100 Pacific Highway, North Sydney NSW 2060
www.randomhouse.com.au

First published by Random House Australia in 2013

Addresses for companies within the Random House Group can be found at
www.randomhouse.com.au/offices

National Library of Australia
Cataloguing-in-Publication Entry

Author: Spratt, R. A.
Title: Nanny Piggins and the Race to Power
ISBN: 978 1 74275 499 4 (pbk.)
Series: Nanny Piggins; 8.
Target Audience: For primary school age
Dewey Number: A823.4

Cover illustration by Gypsy Taylor
Cover design by Christabella Designs
Internal design by Jobi Murphy
Internal illustrations by R. A. Spratt
Typeset in Adobe Garamond by Midland Typesetters, Australia
Printed in Australia by Griffin Press, an Accredited ISO AS/NZS 14001:2004
Environmental Management System printer.

Random House Australia uses papers that are natural, renewable and recyclable products and
made from wood grown in sustainable forests. The logging and manufacturing processes are
expected to conform to the environmental regulations of the country of origin.

# CONTENTS

# CONTENTS

# CHAPTER 1

## Mr Green has a Terrible Idea

Nanny Piggins and the children were just putting the finishing touches on the leaning tower of Pisa. Obviously, it was not the real leaning tower of Pisa. It was a ten-foot-tall replica they had made entirely out of profiteroles, which was no easy thing. As any architect will tell you, twelfth-century Roman-esque columns and Corinthian capitals are hard enough to craft out of stone (hence the lean in the leaning tower), but to make them entirely out

1

of cream, choux pastry and chocolate takes real artistry.

'Finished!' announced Nanny Piggins as she stood back and admired her work.

'It is spectacular,' said Samantha.

'Really impressive,' agreed Derrick.

'Delicious looking,' added Michael.

'I know,' said Nanny Piggins. 'It's a wonder the Italians didn't have the good sense to build the Tower of Pisa out of chocolate and pastry in the first place. That way, when it started to lean they could have eaten it and built it again.'

'Speaking of which,' said Michael, 'can we eat it now? We've got to catch the school bus in twenty minutes and I'm getting hungry.'

'Of course,' said Nanny Piggins. 'We just need to carry it through to the dining room.'

'Can't we eat it here in the kitchen?' asked Samantha, looking at the precariously balanced pillar of food.

'Samantha Green!' exclaimed Nanny Piggins. 'How can you suggest such a thing?! We may be hungry but we are not animals.'

'You are,' Derrick pointed out.

'That's not the point,' said Nanny Piggins. 'When you create a masterpiece of culinary delight such as this, it is too good to be scoffed on the kitchen floor. It needs to be consumed with the elegance and dignity of the dining room.'

'Really?' asked Michael.

'Besides,' said Nanny Piggins, 'I thought if we ate it in the dining room, we could all lie on the dining-room floor and get Boris to push the tower on top of us. Then we could pretend we're earthquake victims forced to bravely eat our way out of the rubble.'

This sounded like a tremendous idea to the children. Apart from involving a delicious breakfast, they suspected that if a ten-foot-tall pillar of food fell on them, there was a very good chance that by the time they ate their way out, they would have missed the bus to school. And Nanny Piggins had very strict rules about not running to catch the school bus. She felt it only gave the bus driver an exaggerated sense of his own importance.

Soon all four of them were carefully carrying the profiterole creation into the dining room. It wobbled with every step, but Nanny Piggins knew more about structural engineering than the twelfth-century Italians, so she'd had the good sense to build in solid chocolate reinforcements to ensure the integrity of the structure. Obviously it takes a great deal of concentration to carry a ten-foot-tall tower of profiteroles. You have to carefully avoid light fittings, doorframes and tripping over your own feet. So, just as they were about to heave the tower onto the table on the count of three, the absolute last thing they wanted to hear was someone loudly clearing their throat.

'Achem,' said the voice loudly.

'Agh!' exclaimed Nanny Piggins as all four of them flinched and the tower wobbled precariously. 'Someone's broken in and is trying to eat our profiteroles! Don't worry, children. I'll distract them while you try to eat as much as you can!'

'Piggins,' said the voice.

'Hang on,' said Nanny Piggins, adjusting her grip on the tower so she could peer around and see the source of the noise. 'Ugh, it's just your father.'

The children groaned. They carefully put down the tower.

'What are you doing here?' demanded Nanny Piggins.

'It's my house,' said Mr Green. 'I've every right to be here at breakfast time.'

'Perhaps,' conceded Nanny Piggins begrudgingly, 'but usually you go to the office early so you can steal other people's food out of the refrigerator and eat that for breakfast.'

Mr Green blushed slightly at this because it was true and he had no idea how his nanny could possibly have found out. (In fact, she had just guessed. When it came to food, Nanny Piggins had the instincts of a criminal profiler. Having worked in the circus for years, she could recognise the many hues of guilt written across a man's face.)

'Anyway, I wanted to speak to you all because I have wonderful news,' said Mr Green.

The children groaned again. Whenever their father had 'wonderful news', it nearly always involved him trying to send them to a workhouse, sell them into slavery or give them to a pack of wild wolves to raise.

'What sort of wonderful news?' said Nanny Piggins, squinting and getting ready to launch herself at his shins.

'I have arranged a holiday for you all in South America,' declared Mr Green.

'Really?' asked Samantha. She was surprised because that sounded rather nice and it was unlike her father to do anything nice.

'Yes, you are all going to stay at a mountain homestead in Chile,' said Mr Green.

'What's the catch?' asked Nanny Piggins.

'No catch,' said Mr Green. 'Just a delightful

holiday for my children, a chance to soak up the local culture and enjoy the sunshine.'

'Are you telling me you went to a travel agent and bought aeroplane tickets yourself, with cash money?' asked Nanny Piggins.

'Yes,' said Mr Green, 'and frankly I resent the implication that you think otherwise.'

'Your own cash money?' asked Nanny Piggins.

'Well . . .' said Mr Green. There was something about Nanny Piggins. When she glared into his eyes, he found it very difficult to lie (and he was normally very good at lying; after all, he was a tax lawyer).

'Who paid for the tickets?' demanded Nanny Piggins.

'The mountain homestead,' admitted Mr Green.

'Why?' demanded Nanny Piggins.

'It's a banana plantation. They paid for the tickets in exchange for six months hard labour,' explained Mr Green.

'You sold your children into slavery for the price of return air tickets?' accused Nanny Piggins.

'No,' admitted Mr Green. 'They are one-way air tickets. They're going to have to work for another six months if they want to come back.'

'Right, that's it! I'm biting him!' declared Nanny Piggins.

The children grabbed hold of Nanny Piggins before she could lunge. They knew she would be cross with herself if she ruined her appetite on their father's trouser leg when there was so much profiterole to look forward to.

'What's this all about, Father?' asked Derrick. 'It's been months since you last tried to get rid of us. Why are you trying to get us out of the way now?'

'Can't a father give his children the gift of hard work, travel and all the bananas you can eat?' asked Mr Green.

Nanny Piggins lurched towards him.

'You'd better tell the truth, Father,' urged Samantha. 'You know how talk of fruit enrages Nanny Piggins. We can't hold her back for much longer.'

'It's none of your business!' snapped Mr Green. 'You're not the boss of me! I don't have to tell you anything!' Mr Green desperately lunged for the door.

'Not one of those three statements is correct!' retorted Nanny Piggins as she athletically lunged for Mr Green.

Unfortunately Mr Green misjudged the width of his own hips (something that often happens to people who eat too many stolen yoghurts from the office refrigerator). He banged the table and the whole profiterole leaning tower of Pisa collapsed on Nanny Piggins and the children before they had a chance to stop him. So Mr Green made good his escape. If lying under a collapsed tower of profiteroles had not been exactly how Nanny Piggins wanted to spend the morning, she would have been quite cross.

Eating a ten-foot-tall profiterole tower is, of course, a process that cannot be rushed. And cleaning all the chocolate stains off your school uniform afterwards is even more time consuming. So, naturally, by the time the children set out for school, the bus was long gone and they had to walk.

'I'm not sure about this,' said Nanny Piggins. 'I don't like letting you go to school when your father is clearly up to something.'

'Don't worry,' urged Derrick. 'Knowing Father, it is probably something trivial.'

'Like he's trying to change his identity to get out of paying a library fine,' guessed Michael.

'Hmm,' said Nanny Piggins. 'I don't know. Your father always looks a little weaselish. But this morning he looked extra specially weaselish. I think he's up to something.'

As they were talking they had made slow progress down the road. They had not gone too far because feet seem heavier when you're walking to school than when you're walking home, particularly if you've got maths first up. Then your feet practically seem to stick to the pavement. Plus, they were all lost in thought as they tried to imagine what devilish tricks Mr Green was up to. So they did not immediately notice that many of the houses in their street had large colour placards in their front gardens, featuring a big photograph of a smiling man.

'Hey, who is that?' asked Michael. 'He looks familiar.'

Nanny Piggins, Derrick and Samantha looked about and noticed the placards as well.

'He does look familiar,' agreed Nanny Piggins. 'That ugly grey suit, the thinning greased-back hair and the unsightly untrimmed eyebrows are all strangely reminiscent of somebody . . .'

They peered closer. Then suddenly Nanny Piggins leapt back, screaming, 'Waaah!'

'What is it?' asked Derrick.

'It's your father!' exclaimed Nanny Piggins.

'Where?' asked Samantha.

'On the poster!' said Nanny Piggins.

'No!' said all three Green children as they stared at the poster again.

'He looks different because he's smiling,' said

Nanny Piggins, 'but if I cover his mouth –' Nanny Piggins put her trotter over the mouth on the poster.

'Aaaggghhh!' screamed all three Green children.

'It *is* him!' exclaimed Derrick.

'What's he doing smiling in a photograph?' asked Samantha.

'I didn't know he could smile,' said Michael. 'I always thought he had some sort of paralysis of the face.'

'But this poster says he's running for mayor!' exclaimed Derrick.

At this point all four of them sat down on the pavement and started eating profiteroles. Fortunately Nanny Piggins had the foresight to stuff her pockets full before they left the house. Nanny Piggins believed it was very important to consume sticky desserts if you had just received a nasty shock.

'But it doesn't make any sense,' said Samantha. 'Father doesn't like doing things.'

'Or drawing attention to himself,' added Derrick.

'Or talking to people,' added Michael.

'And smiling is so unlike him,' said Samantha.

'Does your father have an identical twin brother?' asked Nanny Piggins. 'I often find that is the explanation if I see a horrifying, publicly displayed picture of myself.'

'No,' said Derrick. 'At least I don't think so.'

'But until today I didn't know that Father could smile,' said Samantha, 'so who knows what other dark secrets he has.'

'Well, there's nothing for it,' said Nanny Piggins as she got to her feet and dusted off her designer dress. 'There's no way you can go to school now.'

'Why not?' asked Samantha. (Not that she wanted to go. She just liked to be briefed on whatever complicated excuse Nanny Piggins was going to tell the school secretary.)

'Education may be important, although I'm not one hundred per cent convinced that's true, no matter how much Headmaster Pimplestock yells at me,' said Nanny Piggins. 'But it is much more important to stamp out political disaster.'

'It is?' asked Michael.

'If only Karl Marx's nanny had the good sense to tell him off and make him get a proper job,' said Nanny Piggins. 'A good deal of trouble could have been avoided in the twentieth century.'

'What are we going to do?' asked Derrick.

'According to this poster there is a public meeting at lunchtime today where all the candidates will announce their plans,' said Nanny Piggins.

'So we're going straight to that?' asked Samantha.

'Goodness no,' said Nanny Piggins. 'We've got to go to the bakery first. If I'm going to wrestle your father to the ground, wrench a microphone out of his hands and give him a good telling off, I will need to have a little snack first to give me energy. I'm just glad I had the foresight to put my hot-pink wrestling leotard on under my dress when I got up this morning.'

'Don't you put that on most mornings?' asked Michael.

'Yes, it's uncanny how I always know when I am going to have to wrestle someone that day,' agreed Nanny Piggins.

So after a couple of dozen lemon tarts at Hans' Bakery, Nanny Piggins and the children made their way to the public meeting.

It was the usual dusty, poorly lit building you find in most municipalities. For some reason church halls and community halls always smell unhappy. Most adults have unhappy memories of being forced to participate in a nativity play, or ballet class, or karate lessons in such a hall. Even though the room usually has no furniture, they still somehow have the unpleasant faint aroma of mould, dust and cockroaches. For this occasion, there were a couple of hundred folding chairs set out, but only a few dozen people sitting among them. If you discounted the mayor's staff, family members and vagrants who had come in for a nap and a free doughnut, there were very few people in the audience indeed.

And who could blame the voters of Dulsford? It was an unimpressive line-up. The incumbent, Mayor Bloomsbridge, had been in the position for eight years so everyone knew full well he was a big windbag. Running against him was a shopkeeper who did not like that the council had put a parking meter outside her shop, and finally there was Mr Green. Luckily for Nanny Piggins and the children they did not have to sit through the other two speakers because Mr Green was scheduled to speak first.

'Good afternoon,' said Mr Green. 'My name is Lysander Green.'

The crowd sniggered. There is something about the name 'Lysander'. Like someone burping unexpectedly, it makes even the most intelligent adult giggle.

'I have been a leading tax lawyer in this town for many years.' Mr Green looked over his glasses at the audience, expecting them to be impressed. They were not. As soon as he said the words 'tax lawyer' most people immediately started willing themselves to sleep.

'And I am running for mayor because I want to see –' continued Mr Green.

'Stop right there!' said Nanny Piggins, leaping to her trotters.

This caught the audience's attention. Even the people who had fallen asleep in a doughnut-induced haze snapped awake at the prospect of a good yelling match.

'First of all, before we allow you to continue I want to be clear – are you in fact you, or your own identical twin brother posing as Mr Green as part of some diabolical plot to subvert the natural order?' demanded Nanny Piggins.

'What are you doing here?' responded Mr Green. 'Why aren't the children in school?'

'Don't change the subject!' accused Nanny Piggins. 'If you are an imposter it is a good job I kept the children out of school because the police will need to take a sample of their blood for DNA testing.'

'Would you go home immediately!' hissed Mr Green. 'These are important political proceedings. No-one wants them to be interrupted by a pig!'

'Yes we do!' heckled a politics student in the back row, who was very happy that her essay on local government was going to be a lot more fun to write than she had imagined.

'But if you are the real Mr Green, why on earth are you running for public office?' asked Nanny Piggins.

'Because I have ideas to improve this city. I have lived here all my life and I want to serve the community,' declared Mr Green.

The audience clapped. Usually people only ran for mayor because they were angry about parking meters or not being allowed to cut down the trees in their garden.

'I don't believe a word of it,' said Nanny Piggins. 'You must have a secret despicable motive.'

'How dare you!' spluttered Mr Green.

'If you just admitted you only wanted to be mayor because you'd figured out a way to siphon off council funds into an offshore bank account to fund your expensive Brylcreem habit,' argued Nanny Piggins, 'I might actually have respect for your initiative and give you my vote. After all, to have a despicable, morally bankrupt tax lawyer diverting public money would be marginally better than having to put up with this blathering windbag for another four years.' Nanny Piggins pointed at Mayor Bloomsbridge.

This drew more applause and even cheers from the audience.

'Hey!' complained Mayor Bloomsbridge. He was not good at quick retorts.

'I don't expect a pig like you to understand,' said Mr Green, 'but I want to make this city better for my children and my children's children.'

Nanny Piggins gasped. 'Now that is just a big fat lie. If you care so much about your children, I challenge you to name any one of their favourite cakes.'

'Um . . . er . . . this is ridiculous,' blathered Mr Green.

'You can't, can you?' denounced Nanny Piggins.

'Chocolate cake. Their favourite is chocolate cake!' yelled Mr Green desperately.

Nanny Piggins scowled at him for a moment. 'That question was too easy. Everyone likes chocolate cake the best.'

At this point two burly security guards grabbed hold of Nanny Piggins and tried to drag her out. Fortunately she'd had the good sense to sew velcro into her designer ensemble, so she quickly whipped her dress off, revealing her hot-pink wrestling leotard underneath, then proceeded to give a 35-minute demonstration on mixed martial arts. Neither of the other two candidates got to speak, and before long the Police Sergeant arrived, lured Nanny Piggins into his squad car with a chocolate biscuit and drove her home.

'I just don't understand it,' said Nanny Piggins as she shoved another profiterole in her mouth (she had made a Taj Mahal of profiteroles when she got home to overcome the ordeal). 'Why on earth would your father run for mayor?'

'Perhaps he does want to serve the community,' suggested Samantha.

'I doubt it,' said Nanny Piggins. 'He'd have to have some sort of brain-altering stroke to have such a radical change of character. If that happened there would be other symptoms, like dribbling or slurred speech. And I haven't noticed your father doing any more of that than usual.'

'Perhaps he has a guilty conscience about all the wicked things he's done,' guessed Boris.

'If he had a guilty conscience the first thing he would do,' said Nanny Piggins, 'is stop being wicked.

And I know he hasn't done that because I saw him steal Mrs Simpson's newspaper off her nature strip this morning.'

'Perhaps he wants to be mayor so he can get loads more tax deductions,' guessed Michael.

The others nodded as they pondered this. It was the first explanation that made any sense. Mr Green did love tax deductions.

'He'd be able to claim all the dry-cleaning for the mayor's robes,' said Michael.

'And he'd be able to stop getting his suit dry-cleaned because the mayoral robes would cover all the stains,' agreed Nanny Piggins.

'It sounds like an awful lot of trouble to go to just to avoid paying his dry-cleaning bill,' said Samantha.

'Hmm,' said Nanny Piggins, 'I agree. I suspect your father is up to something even more weaselish.'

'Does one of your extra pig senses detect weaselishness?' asked Derrick.

'No,' said Nanny Piggins, 'but my familiarity with your father does.'

DING-DONG.

The doorbell rang.

'Who could that be?' asked Nanny Piggins.

'Perhaps it's the Police Sergeant,' suggested

Samantha. 'He did drop his handcuffs in the kitchen when he was wrestling with you to stop you going back to the public meeting, then wrestling with you to let him have some of your shortbread biscuits.'

'Sometimes I think he drops his police equipment here on purpose so he's got an excuse to come back and get more biscuits,' said Nanny Piggins as she got up to answer the door.

But when she swung the door open, it was not her dear friend from the police force. It was a scrawny lower-level bureaucrat from the local council.

'Good afternoon, madam,' said the scrawny bureaucrat. 'I am here today to inform you of a development proposal for your local area. A new freeway is going to be built two kilometres west of your house, which the council is legally obliged to inform you may have a 14 per cent effect on the through traffic in your street.'

'Sorry,' said Nanny Piggins. 'What did you say? I didn't hear anything after you rudely labelled me "madam".'

'I apologise,' said the lower-level bureaucrat. 'Would you prefer Ms?'

'I would not!' declared Nanny Piggins. 'I prefer to be addressed by my full title, Doctor Nanny Piggins – World's Greatest Flying Pig.'

'Doctor?' questioned Derrick. 'You're not a doctor.'

'Yes I am,' said Nanny Piggins. 'I have an honorary doctorate from the University of North Carolina. It's where the Wright brothers invented the aeroplane, so they appreciate my contribution to flight.'

The bureaucrat handed Nanny Piggins a leaflet. 'Everything you need to know about the new motorway is in here,' he said. 'If you have any questions, you can call our helpline.'

'If I do call your helpline will I be forced to listen to cheaply recorded classical music, punctuated every 45 seconds by a pre-recorded lie that my call is important to you and if I just hold the line the first available operator will be with me shortly?' asked Nanny Piggins.

'Probably,' admitted the scrawny bureaucrat.

'Then you can answer my questions now,' said Nanny Piggins. 'When is this motorway going to be built?'

'Next year,' said the scrawny bureaucrat, 'after the council holds discussions with the community they will decide on the exact route.'

Suddenly the scrawny bureaucrat had her full attention.

'Are you telling me that the mayor will get to decide where this motorway goes?' asked Nanny Piggins.

'After a public consultation process, yes,' said the scrawny bureaucrat.

'No wonder your father is running for mayor!' exclaimed Nanny Piggins. 'I knew he was up to something.'

Sadly, with his terrible lack of timing, Mr Green chose that exact moment to pull up in his Rolls-Royce.

'You!' accused Nanny Piggins as he got out of the car. 'What are you up to? Why do you want to control the course of the new motorway? Are you going to divert it to cover over a hole in the woods where you bury all your old tax returns so the tax office can never discover what wickedness you've been up to?'

'Yagh!' yelped Mr Green. He did not know what to be more shocked by. The fact that his nanny had figured out his plans to divert a motorway or the fact that his nanny knew that he buried his incriminating tax returns in a hole in the woods.

'What are you planning?' demanded Nanny Piggins.

The bureaucrat took the opportunity to run

away. (Sadly he ran immediately next door where Mrs McGill was even meaner to him.)

Mr Green looked about at the accusing glares of his children and decided the jig was up. While he had always been excellent at lying in general, he had never been good at lying when he had to make eye contact. He'd received a D in the subject when he'd had to study it at law school.

'All right, all right,' said Mr Green. 'I decided to run for mayor after I heard about the new motorway. I thought I could really cash in.'

'How?' asked Nanny Piggins.

'I could get the motorway to run right through our house,' explained Mr Green. 'The council would have to buy us out. Then I could buy a much cheaper one-bedroom flat in the city and pocket a fortune.'

'But where would the children live?' asked Nanny Piggins.

'I don't know, I was hoping a banana plantation in Chile,' said Mr Green. 'Aren't they old enough to leave home yet?'

'Are you old enough to leave home yet?' demanded Nanny Piggins. 'Sometimes I wonder if it is you who should stay at home and be monitored fulltime by a trained professional.'

'Anyway, now you know,' said Mr Green, 'I was

wondering if you could do a couple of things to help with my campaign?'

'What?' asked Nanny Piggins.

'You know, print off some leaflets, put up some signs, write a few speeches, doorknock the neighbourhood and tell everyone to vote for me?' asked Mr Green.

'You mean you want Nanny Piggins to run your whole campaign for you?' asked Samantha.

'Well, yes,' said Mr Green. 'All that talking to people isn't really my cup of tea. And I've got to get to work. So I'll leave it to you to handle all that.'

'You will do no such thing,' declared Nanny Piggins.

'What?' spluttered Mr Green. 'But that's insubordination.'

'Too right it is,' agreed Nanny Piggins. 'Not only will I not help you, I intend to thwart you in every way.'

'Oh, come on now,' said Mr Green. 'There's no need for that.'

'I shall not let you divert a motorway to destroy the children's home. And I shall not let you become mayor and hold one iota of power over anybody in this town,' denounced Nanny Piggins. 'You are a small-minded, selfish, weaselly man, and while normally that would make you perfectly suited to be a politician, on this occasion I refuse to allow it.'

'I don't see how you can stop me,' challenged Mr Green.

'I shall stop you,' said Nanny Piggins, 'by running for mayor myself and trouncing you in the local elections!'

There was a moment of complete silence, before Mr Green burst out laughing.

'What are you laughing at?' demanded Nanny Piggins.

'As if anybody would ever vote for you!' he laughed. 'You're a pig!'

The children winced.

'We shall see,' said Nanny Piggins in a menacingly quiet voice. 'Come election day you will discover whether the people of Dulsford would rather be represented by a pig or a tax lawyer.'

'They might vote for the incumbent mayor,' said Derrick.

'Or the shopkeeper who doesn't like parking meters,' said Michael.

'Pish,' said Nanny Piggins. 'I'll soon deal with them.'

'But the election is only two months away,' blustered Mr Green. 'You haven't got time to launch a proper campaign now. You missed the first event today.'

'Two months is more than enough time for me to convince the voters in this city that you are a weaselly good-for-nothing and I am Nanny Piggins, World's Greatest Flying Pig!' declared Nanny Piggins.

'But you *are* Nanny Piggins, World's Greatest Flying Pig,' said Michael, slightly confused.

'Exactly,' agreed Nanny Piggins, 'which is why it will be so easy to convince people.'

'Please don't,' pleaded Mr Green. 'I know I can beat the mayor because I have a copy of his tax return, which is very incriminating. But if you get involved it is only going to make everything more complicated and theatrical.'

'Nothing you could say could convince me to change my mind,' declared Nanny Piggins.

'I'll buy you a chocolate cake,' said Mr Green.

Nanny Piggins visibly flinched.

'Oooh,' said Derrick, impressed by his father's ingenuity, 'perhaps Father would make a good politician after all.'

Nanny Piggins wrestled against her instinctive lust for cake for a few seconds before the greater good won out. 'No amount of cake could make me change my mind,' she said. 'I don't want your cake!'

The children gasped. They had never heard her utter such words before.

'What about . . . a leaning tower of Pisa of cake,' asked Mr Green, 'like that profiterole tower you had this morning?'

Nanny Piggins shuddered. She really had to battle her hungry side now.

'Never,' she cried.

'What about a leaning tower of Pisa of cake that wasn't a scale model,' said Mr Green. 'One that was life sized – over 50 metres tall.'

Nanny Piggins grasped Derrick and Samantha for support. Her knees were buckling at the thought of so much delicious cake.

'You're lying. There's no way you could get your hands on such a cake,' Nanny Piggins whispered.

'Yes I could,' said Mr Green. 'I do the tax return for the Slimbridge Cake Factory too. I know they over-claimed on their chocolate chip shipments. I can bend them to my will and their ovens could bake a cake of monumental proportions.'

Nanny Piggins closed her eyes and reached deep within herself for every ounce of her considerable courage. 'No!' she said, 'No, no, no! I will not let you become mayor. And if I have to defy my natural instinct to be a reckless cake-eating maverick and instead assume the responsibility of high office, then that is what I shall do. Good day, sir.'

Nanny Piggins stepped back and slammed the front door closed in Mr Green's face.

'You realise you just shut Father out of his own house?' asked Michael.

'It seemed the appropriate thing to do,' explained Nanny Piggins. 'When you have worked in the circus for as long as I did, you get wonderful instincts for these dramatic gestures. Besides, he can come around and let himself in the back door if he wants to.'

'So are you really going to run for mayor?' asked Samantha.

'It looks like it,' said Nanny Piggins, 'but don't worry. Beating your father will be simple. I'll just turn up at a few events looking glamorous and easily trounce him. It won't affect my nannying duties at all.'

The children were not so sure.

# CHAPTER 2

## Nanny Piggins and the Campaign Strategy

Nanny Piggins, Boris and the children were exhausted. It was only 6 o'clock in the morning but they had been up all night making cake. And unlike all the other occasions when Nanny Piggins stayed up all night making cake, on this occasion she had not eaten any (at least, not very much) because she was not making them for herself, she was making her cakes for the voters. Her plan was to go door-to-door handing out cake. Traditionally, would-be politicians go door-to-door explaining their policies and making political promises. But Nanny Piggins thought voters were much more likely to be swayed by a chocolate mud cake. So they were all sitting around the kitchen table jamming the last of the silver balls into the inch-thick chocolate icing on the last of the two thousand cakes they had made during the course of the night.

'There are thirty thousand people living in Dulsford,' said Samantha. 'Are you really intending to make another 28,000 cakes?'

'Oh yes,' said Nanny Piggins. 'If we make two thousand a night that will only take us two weeks.'

'But we're all exhausted now, just from making these cakes,' said Derrick, 'and we haven't even gone out and delivered them all yet. I don't know if we can keep this up.'

'Euaaaah euaah,' said Michael. He was snoring because he was only seven years old and had fallen asleep sometime around three in the morning in the middle of spreading cream and jam across the centre of a cake. Luckily his face had fallen sideways as he collapsed across the table, so the cream-covered sponge was actually providing him with a very comfortable pillow.

'Well, on average, about three per cent of people

are diabetic, so it would be irresponsible to give them a slice of cake. I'll give them tickets to the circus instead,' continued Nanny Piggins. 'Then we can also exclude people we don't like, such as Nanny Anne and Headmaster Pimplestock. I refuse to give them anything. Then we only have to make another 27,088 cakes. So that isn't so bad at all.'

The children did not say anything, partly because they were too tired and partly because there was no reasoning with Nanny Piggins when it came to maths, it was like talking to an Eskimo in Swahili. Luckily they were saved from forcing their sluggish minds to form reasoned arguments by a knock at the door.

'Who could that be?' asked Boris.

'It's six o'clock in the morning,' added Derrick.

'Perhaps it's the milkman come to apologise for forgetting to leave the 14,000 sticks of butter I asked for,' guessed Nanny Piggins.

'Perhaps it's someone else who's been up all night baking cakes,' guessed Samantha, 'and they've come over to borrow a cup of sugar.'

'I'd better answer the door right away then,' said Nanny Piggins, leaping to her feet and picking up a bag of sugar. 'There's nothing worse than having your butter all measured out, then discovering there's no sugar to cream it with.'

The children followed as soon as they could. It took a moment because their legs were paralysed from having been sitting making cake for so long. So they reached the hallway just as Nanny Piggins flung open the front door.

'What type of cake are you baking? Chocolate? Caramel? Lemon drizzle?' asked Nanny Piggins collegially. But the words soon died on her lips, because the woman in front of her was clearly not the type to bake cakes. She was dressed in a grey office suit, stylish thin-framed glasses and a sleek fashionable haircut (the type that looks like you did nothing to it at all but really takes 45 minutes with a blow-dryer to achieve). She was rather short, but also extremely attractive, which is a look that is hard to pull off at six o'clock in the morning.

'What do you want?' asked Nanny Piggins, immediately on the defensive. She distrusted anybody who was well dressed before 10 am, unless they had not been to bed yet, but even then they should be slightly dishevelled from a long night of dancing.

'I'm here to help you,' said the professional-looking woman. 'My name is Tyler Forrest and I'm your new campaign manager.'

'Hmm,' said Nanny Piggins, 'I do like a woman

with confidence. But there is a threshold of over-confidence beyond which I instinctively want to stomp on your foot, and you seem to have taken a giant leap over that threshold. You might want to be my campaign manager but you aren't because I haven't hired you.'

'But you will,' said Tyler. 'Once you let me explain, you'll see that you have no chance of winning without me. But if you hire me, we could go all the way, not just to mayor, but we could take this national – one day you could be prime minister.'

'I just want to thwart Mr Green,' said Nanny Piggins. 'I don't want the responsibility of running an entire country. I already have a job looking after these three children. I know I'm good at multi-tasking but I'm not that good.'

'No matter,' said Tyler. 'I will help you achieve this limited goal, for now.'

'Why?' asked Derrick.

'I work for the Emily Davison Electoral Society dedicated to supporting women running for public office,' explained Tyler.

'You do realise that Nanny Piggins is a pig?' asked Samantha.

'We're prepared to overlook that,' conceded Tyler. 'To be honest, we have a hard time finding potential candidates. Most women have too much sense to want to be involved in politics, which is why we must redouble our efforts and throw them behind the silly ones.'

'That's all very well,' said Nanny Piggins, 'but I don't need you. I already have a brilliant electoral strategy. I'm going to give everyone in the electorate . . .'

'Excluding diabetics and meanies,' added Derrick.

'Yes, excluding them,' agreed Nanny Piggins. 'I'm going to give them all a cake.' Nanny Piggins smiled proudly at the ingeniousness of her brilliant idea.

'Is that it?' asked Tyler.

'What do you mean "is that it?"' asked Nanny Piggins. 'Do you have any idea how good my cakes are?'

'I'm sure they're delicious,' said Tyler, 'but your plan will never work. You've already tied up the cake-loving vote because your dedication to cake and cake-related causes is well known throughout the town. But people who don't like cake or, more seriously, don't like themselves because of how much they *do* like cake, will only resent you if you give them a delicious, calorie-laden treat.'

Nanny Piggins gasped. 'You mean . . . I'll be undone by dieters?!'

'Precisely,' said Tyler. 'And at any given time as many as 93 per cent of the population think they are on a diet. That figure actually goes up immediately after Christmas.'

'What do you mean "think they are on a diet"?' asked Derrick.

'Ninety per cent of people tell themselves they are on a diet,' explained Tyler, 'but actually only two or three per cent of those people actually eat less. It's a complex psychological conditional called "kidding yourself".'

'I see,' said Derrick, which was actually an example of 'kidding himself' because really he did not.

'Anyway, if anyone who thinks they are on a diet finds a delicious chocolate mud cake in their letterbox, they will eat it, then they will be cross with themselves for eating it, then they will get cross at the person who gave it to them,' continued Tyler. 'There will be a massive electoral backlash and you'll lose in a landslide.'

'Oh dear,' said Nanny Piggins. 'It's horrifying to think that so much wonderful cake could cause so much unhappiness.'

'Which is why you need to triangulate,' explained Tyler.

'Triangu-whatie?' asked Nanny Piggins.

'Triangulate,' said Tyler. 'It is an ingenious electoral strategy invented by former American President Bill Clinton, where you ignore the people who love you because they will love you whatever you do. Then you focus all your energy on pandering to the people who dislike you intensely.'

'But who dislikes Nanny Piggins intensely?' asked Michael. He found it impossible to believe that people could not love his nanny as much as he did.

'Fitness fanatics and healthy eaters,' stated Tyler.

'My Achilles heel,' gasped Nanny Piggins.

'You need to win over the gym junkies,' explained Tyler.

'But to do so would be to go against all my principles, everything I believe in,' said Nanny Piggins.

'It won't be so hard,' argued Tyler. 'You are a flying pig and therefore an elite athlete.'

'True,' agreed Nanny Piggins.

'But that's an extreme sport,' continued Tyler. 'You need to let the fit and healthy know you are one of them.'

'How?' asked Nanny Piggins.

'By taking up jogging,' said Tyler.

'Noooooooooooo!' screamed Nanny Piggins.

Eventually, several minutes later, the children managed to calm Nanny Piggins down again, largely by feeding her several dozen freshly made cakes (which fortuitously were so close at hand).

'I despise those who jog,' said an emotional Nanny Piggins, 'but to do it myself –' she literally shuddered to think of it – 'would be to defile everything I believe in, to betray every cake I have ever eaten.'

'Do you want to be mayor of Dulsford?' asked Tyler.

'Not particularly,' admitted Nanny Piggins.

'Do you want to beat Mr Green, stop him from becoming mayor and ruining everything you don't hate about this city?' asked Tyler.

Nanny Piggins thought about it for a moment. 'Yes, yes I do.'

'Then sacrifices have to be made,' said Tyler. 'In all campaigns, if you are going to win, the first thing that has to go is the candidate's dignity.'

'Pass me a slice of cake,' said Nanny Piggins forlornly. 'If I'm going to take up jogging I shall need the energy.'

'Oh, you're not just going to take up jogging,' said Tyler. 'I've entered you in the Town to Tip fun run.'

At this point Nanny Piggins fainted (or fell asleep, it was hard to tell because she was very tired). Her brain obviously needed to shut down in order to block out the reality that she was now going to take up such a deeply unpleasant sport.

Fortunately, Boris was able to wake his sister by slapping her in the face with a cream pie, which only took him 45 minutes to whip up especially for this purpose.

'But I can't go in a fun run!' protested Nanny Piggins. 'It would go against everything I believe in.'

'Exactly,' agreed Tyler, 'which is how you would win over an entirely new demographic to your campaign.'

'Triangucake,' nodded Boris.

'But there's nothing fun about running,' argued Nanny Piggins, 'unless it's after an ice-cream truck, and even then the fun part is actually catching it, tying up the ice-cream man and eating all his stock.'

'And the Town to Tip run is very hilly,' argued Samantha.

'And it goes right past the Slimbridge Cake Factory,' added Michael. 'Nanny Piggins has never been able to run past that, even in a locked car driving at 80 km an hour. She still finds it impossible to resist the urge to kick out the window and leap out.'

'It's true,' admitted Nanny Piggins. 'It means we have to travel in some very circuitous routes to get about town.'

'That's why you've got to train,' said Tyler. 'You've got an entire week until the race, which is plenty of time to build up your willpower.'

The training regime started at 5 am sharp the next morning, when Nanny Piggins tried climbing out her window and running away, but Tyler was one step ahead of her. As a campaign manager she was used to dealing with politicians who were tremendously morally bankrupt, and always sneaking off to be naughty. So Tyler had the foresight to set up a net at the bottom of the drainpipe.

She soon bundled Nanny Piggins up in the back of Mr Green's Rolls-Royce and drove her down to the athletics track to begin training. The children and Boris got up early and went along too, because they knew they were to see a very rare sight indeed – Nanny Piggins not only taking exercise but also doing as she was told.

Things did not start well. Tyler began by telling Nanny Piggins to do six laps of the field, then she blew a whistle. Nanny Piggins responded by yanking the whistle off Tyler's neck, swinging it around her head and lobbing it up into the gutter of the grand-stand.

'I'm not going anywhere until I've had at least a dozen doughnuts,' said Nanny Piggins, beginning to get that menacing look in her eyes that she always got when she was contemplating violence.

'You're not getting any doughnuts, full stop,' said Tyler, who it turns out was capable of an equally fierce glower. 'If you want to impress healthy people, you will have to stop jamming baked goods in your face at every available opportunity.'

'I'll jam your shin in my mouth in a minute,' threatened Nanny Piggins.

'Ladies, ladies,' said Boris, bravely intervening. (He wasn't *too* brave. He had worn steel-plated shin guards in anticipation of his sister becoming delirious with low blood cake levels and lashing out.) 'Might I suggest a compromise?'

'What?' asked Tyler and Nanny Piggins.

'You want Sarah to go jogging and, Sarah, you want to eat a piece of cake. I anticipated this impasse,' said Boris. (He had been learning some big words at law school.) 'I took the liberty of filling up the boot of the Rolls-Royce with Swiss rolls last night, so Tyler could drive the Rolls-Royce around the track and Sarah could chase it, thereby –'

'There's cake in the Rolls?!' interrupted Nanny Piggins.

Boris didn't answer; he leapt on his sister, pinning her to the ground while flinging the Rolls-Royce keys to Tyler. 'Quick, drive! I'll delay her as long as I can, but I'll only be able to hold her for a few seconds.'

Fortunately Tyler had already taken off running. She snatched the keys out of the air and leapt in through the open window of the Rolls, screeching out onto the track and taking off.

One particularly vicious nipple cripple to her hapless brother later, and Nanny Piggins gave chase. It was an extraordinary sight. Tyler sped around the track all morning and Nanny Piggins never lost pace. She was like a cyborg, ruthlessly, unrelentingly powering after her prey, lap after lap. They didn't stop at ten, they kept going for fifty, then one hundred laps. Nanny Piggins completely focused on the cake and the cake alone.

'Do you think she realises she could have run to Hans' Bakery and back ten times over by now?' asked Michael.

'I don't think she's thinking about anything,' said Boris. 'She can smell the cake in the boot and it's completely overpowered all rational thought in her mind.'

'Does Nanny Piggins have many rational thoughts in her mind?' asked Samantha.

'Not many,' admitted Boris, 'but when she hasn't had any breakfast, there are none at all.'

'Hey look!' said Derrick. 'The Rolls-Royce is slowing down.'

'What's Tyler doing?' asked Boris. 'Doesn't she know she is taking her life in her own hands?'

As the Rolls-Royce swooped past the grandstand, Tyler wound down her window and called out, 'Help me! I'm running out of petrol!'

'Use the little lever in the glove box to pop open the boot!' advised Boris. 'For your own safety you need to placate her with cake.'

So just as the Rolls-Royce glided to a stuttering stop, the boot popped open and Nanny Piggins leapt mouth-first into it. They could not see her, but they could hear her guzzling and they could see the car shuddering as she lashed about inside the boot, gobbling up every last crumb of cake.

Tyler, visibly shocked by the experience, went over to join the others in the grandstand. 'Well I think we've established that Nanny Piggins is already pretty good at running.'

'She's a gifted all-round athlete,' agreed Boris. 'People think being a flying pig is just a case of lying in a cannon waiting for the gunpowder to explode, but once you have been blasted, there's an awful lot of jogging back to the starting point.'

'The hard thing is going to be training her to run past the Slimbridge Cake Factory,' predicted Michael.

'All right,' said Tyler. 'I'll plan tomorrow's training session to focus on that.'

'What are we going to do this afternoon?' asked Derrick.

'I think I'll be spending most of the afternoon at the Rolls-Royce dealership getting it repaired,' said Tyler. 'In her haste to get as much cake in her mouth as possible, I think Nanny Piggins has eaten all the carpet and some of the electrical wiring.'

So the next day's training session started 500 metres down the road from the Slimbridge Cake Factory.

'I don't understand why I have to run past the factory,' said Nanny Piggins. 'I'm sure I could pop in for a couple of dozen cakes, say hello to my dear friends on the assembly line, and still get back on track and win the race.'

'It's not a question of winning or eating cake,' said Tyler.

'Wash your mouth out!' exclaimed Nanny Piggins.

'It's a question of appearances,' continued Tyler. 'You're a politician now. You need to present yourself as a healthy person. And healthy people don't raid cake factories.'

'Mentally healthy people do,' grumbled Nanny Piggins. 'If more people popped in to cake factories there would be more happiness in the world.'

'And more obesity and more diabetes,' chided Tyler.

'I'd rather spend time with a fat diabetic,' declared Nanny Piggins, 'than a miserable skinny bones!'

Tyler sighed. 'Please never say that to anyone in the media.'

'You can do it, Nanny Piggins,' encouraged Michael. 'All you have to do is run from here, straight down the road until you're 500 metres past the factory.'

'It's only 1000 metres all up,' added Derrick. 'You run that all the time.'

'Oh, I know I can do it,' said Nanny Piggins. 'The problem is why should I do it?'

'To beat Father,' reminded Samantha.

'Hmpf,' grumbled Nanny Piggins. 'Attractive as that idea is, it's not as attractive as the reality of a Slimbridge Bavarian Chocolate Cake in my mouth.'

'That's why we've set up a trestle table laden with all of Slimbridge's finest baked goods at the other end,' said Boris.

'How many of their baked goods?' questioned Nanny Piggins.

'Two hundred family-sized cakes,' said Michael.

'Hmm,' said Nanny Piggins. 'All right, I agree to it.'

They all climbed out of the car. Nanny Piggins

shuddered when the sweet smell of cake hit her nostrils.

'You can do it, Nanny Piggins,' urged Samantha.

'Of course I can,' agreed Nanny Piggins.

'Think of the cake at the other end,' advised Michael.

'Run as fast as you can,' encouraged Derrick.

'All right,' said Nanny Piggins. 'Here goes.' With that she took off, sprinting down the road past the cake factory. And she did really well; she got a whole hundred metres down the road before she suddenly broke stride, stopped, then leapt onto the cyclone wire fence and took off into the grounds of the factory.

'I'm impressed she got as far as she did,' said Michael.

Later, after seven security guards dragged her out of the factory, the children reasoned with Nanny Piggins as she sat on the curb finishing up the last of the cake she had managed to stuff in her pockets.

'Why did you do it?' asked Samantha. 'You knew there was plenty of cake waiting for you at the other end.'

'Yes,' agreed Nanny Piggins, 'but this cake was closer and it was calling me.'

'The cake called to you?' asked Tyler.

'Oh yes,' said Nanny Piggins. '*Nanny Piggins, eat me, eat me!* it cried. It would have been rude for me not to respond.'

'You don't really think you can hear cake talking to you, do you?' asked Derrick, beginning to worry about his nanny.

'Of course I do!' said Nanny Piggins. 'I'll admit they don't do it very loudly. But telepathically I can hear what they'd like to say to me loud and clear.'

'I have been running campaigns for fifteen years and I have never come across a problem like this,' said Tyler, also slumping down in the gutter and helping herself to a slice of cake. 'We can motivate Nanny Piggins to run with cake but we can't motivate her to run past a cake factory with cake.' She stuffed an especially large slice of sponge into her mouth to punctuate this thought.

'Good morning, Nanny Piggins.'

They all looked up to see Nanny Piggins' greatest arch nemesis – Nanny Anne (well, her third greatest after the Ringmaster and Eduardo the Flying Armadillo). She was wearing lycra leggings, $400 running shoes and a baby-pink singlet – which all suggested that she was out running, and yet there was not a hair out of place on her head and not a molecule of sweat on her face.

'What are you doing here?' grumbled Nanny Piggins. 'If you're thinking of breaking into the cake factory, there's no point. I've already cleaned them out of all the easy-to-grab supplies.'

Nanny Anne laughed her fake laugh, which sounded like a computer generated approximation of a normal human laugh. 'Oh dear me no, I haven't had a slice of cake for four months now,' said Nanny Anne.

'You poor thing,' said Nanny Piggins. Much as she disliked Nanny Anne as a person, she could not help but be touched by such a sad story.

'I'm in training for the big run on Saturday,' said Nanny Anne smugly.

'You mean the Town to Tip?' asked Derrick.

'Yes,' said Nanny Anne. 'I have written several letters to the organisers asking them to change the name to something more inspiring.'

'Typical,' said Nanny Piggins. 'I should have known you of all people would be a jogger. It takes a certain type of depraved character to stoop so low.'

'And what are you doing here?' asked Nanny Anne, with her sickly sweet smile. 'Are you waiting for the police to pick you up? Or perhaps a mental health professional?'

It shows how strongly Nanny Piggins disliked Nanny Anne that she seriously considered hurling the chunk of chocolate cake in her hand at Nanny Anne's perfectly laundered pink singlet. Fortunately, good sense prevailed and she stuffed it in her mouth instead. 'I'm training for the fun run too,' she muttered, spraying cake crumbs because she ate as she talked (one of her favourite types of multi-tasking).

At this point Nanny Anne really did burst out laughing. She laughed and laughed for a full two minutes, which is a very long time to sit in the gutter watching someone delight at your expense.

'Why are you laughing?' demanded Nanny Piggins.

'Oh, I'm sorry,' said Nanny Anne (although she was not). 'I thought you were joking.'

'Why would I be joking?' demanded Nanny Piggins. 'I am one of the greatest, if not *the* greatest athlete in the entire world. No-one has ever bested me in the field of being blasted out of a cannon.'

Nanny Anne burst out laughing again.

'Why is that funny?' asked Derrick.

Nanny Anne was dabbing away tears now because she was laughing so hard her eyes had started to water. 'Well, being blasted out of a cannon is hardly a real sport, is it?'

THWACK!

The sound of a slice of mud cake hitting Nanny Anne's clothes was a distinctive one. Normally a stain on her outfit would drive Nanny Anne apoplectic with rage, but on this occasion it only made her burst out laughing again.

'Take that back!' demanded Nanny Piggins. 'How dare you insult the art and science of being a flying pig!' Nanny Piggins lunged for Nanny Anne but the children and Boris grabbed her. And Nanny Anne had the good sense to take off jogging down the road.

'Let me at her,' insisted Nanny Piggins.

'If you bite her she'll call the police,' urged Derrick.

'At least let me chase her down and get my slice of cake back,' pleaded Nanny Piggins.

'Let her go,' said Samantha, 'just let her go.'

'But the chocolate filling had real cream,' sobbed Nanny Piggins.

Boris wrapped his sister in a big bear hug. 'Don't worry, if we go back to the factory and knock politely on the door I'm sure they'll give you another slice.'

'That was the last slice,' wept Nanny Piggins.

'Really?' asked Derrick. 'They only had one slice in the entire factory?'

'No, they had sixty slices,' admitted Nanny Piggins, 'but I had to munch on something while I was running away from the guards.'

'Of course,' agreed Boris, patting her hand.

'Well, there is nothing for it,' declared Nanny Piggins, standing up and brushing off her skirt. 'I shall have to beat Nanny Anne on Saturday, and I shall have to run faster than her in the race too.'

From that point on no-one needed to coach Nanny Piggins anymore. She was up before dawn every day, carrying out her own brutal training regimen. Admittedly it did not involve much running. A quick jog down to Hans' bakery, a three-hour session of carbo loading, and then home to rest. But she did it all with such impressive focus and dedication, the children began to believe that perhaps being only four foot tall would not stop their nanny from winning the Town to Tip.

The big day arrived. Nanny Piggins came downstairs, dressed ready for the race.

'Why are you wearing your hot-pink wrestling leotard?' asked Derrick.

'Just in case,' said Nanny Piggins cryptically.

'You're planning to wrestle Nanny Anne, aren't you?' guessed Samantha.

'I'd like to be prepared should the eventuality occur,' said Nanny Piggins as she tucked into a hearty breakfast of chocolate croissants.

'But you've got to wear your campaign t-shirt,' said Tyler, pulling out a fluorescent green t-shirt featuring a picture of Nanny Piggins jogging and the slogan, '*A Vote for Piggins is a Vote for Good Health.*'

'That is the ugliest t-shirt I've ever seen,' denounced Nanny Piggins. 'Which designer made this for you? Let me know and I shall call Paris immediately to tear strips off them!'

'It wasn't made by a European designer,' said Tyler. 'It was made by Larry from the Copy Shack.'

'But I don't wear clothes made by Larry,' said Nanny Piggins, 'unless you count Yves Saint Laurent. But he prefers it if I only call him Larry when none of his designer friends is around.'

'Wearing a simple t-shirt will make you look like one of the people,' urged Tyler. 'The voters will like it.'

And so with great reluctance Nanny Piggins was driven to the starting line wearing the hideous green t-shirt. As soon as she got out of the car Nanny Piggins started being difficult.

'Ew, I can't go through with it!' proclaimed Nanny Piggins. 'I can't run!'

'What's wrong now?' sighed Tyler.

'The smell!' complained Nanny Piggins. 'It's dreadful. I've never smelt so much menthol rub in the air.'

Even the children had to admit the other runners were a bit pongy. You did not need a super sensitive pig snout to be able to sniff them a mile away.

'Come on, Sarah,' urged Boris as he tried dragging her towards the marshalling area. 'You've got to do it. We all got up at 5.30 this morning to get you here on time. And there's nowhere else to go because the sweet shop doesn't open for another three hours.'

'I won't do it!' screamed Nanny Piggins, opening her mouth wide to chomp on her brother's shin.

'Good morning, Nanny Piggins,' said Nanny Anne. 'Are you being attacked by that bear? Would you like me to call Animal Control?'

'I'll call Human Control and have you taken away in a van if you don't watch out,' cried Nanny Piggins.

'There's no such thing as Human Control,' whispered Michael.

'Well, there should be,' said Nanny Piggins. 'Some people shouldn't be allowed to roam the streets without wearing a leash.'

'Good morning, Piggins,' said Mr Green.

'What are you doing here?' demanded Nanny Piggins. 'Is this what all unpleasant people do? Get up first thing in the morning and go jogging?'

'I've come to watch,' said Mr Green smugly. 'As the future mayor I must be seen to participate in community events.'

'By participate you mean sit on the sidelines doing nothing, don't you,' said Nanny Piggins.

'I believe in small government,' said Mr Green. 'Doing nothing is my policy platform.'

'Come on, Nanny Piggins,' urged Derrick. 'You'd better make your way over to the starting line. They're about to begin.'

So Nanny Piggins went and lined up with all the health and fitness fanatics of Dulsford, as well as the people taking part in the race 'just for a laugh'. They made Nanny Piggins feel saddest of all. Anyone who finds running ten kilometres funny clearly is a troubled soul. Nanny Piggins made a mental note to send cake to all these people as soon as she became mayor.

BANG!

The race began and everyone took off. Nanny Anne started at a brisk pace at the front of the pack. But Nanny Piggins sprinted away at lightning speed.

'She'll never be able to keep up that pace,' said Derrick.

'Why not?' asked Boris. 'It's not like she didn't do enough carbo-loading.'

'But it's ten kilometres,' said Michael. 'That's a long way.'

'Pish!' said Boris (quoting his sister). 'Once, during a twenty-minute interval at the circus, Nanny Piggins decided she fancied a cupcake, so she ran sixteen kilometres to the nearest supermarket for a bag of flour, ran back, whipped up a batch of cupcakes and ate them.'

'In under twenty minutes?!' marvelled Michael.

'Well it did take her a little longer,' admitted Boris, 'but the Ringmaster was very understanding about it. He held up the show to wait for her.'

The children and Boris were able to follow the race on a huge jumbotron TV screen that had been set up in the town square.

'She's coming up to the cake factory,' worried Samantha.

They watched Nanny Piggins start rifling in the pockets of her hot-pink wrestling leotard (she had pockets sewn into it so that she would never be without a chocolate bar when wrestling).

'What's she doing?' wondered Derrick.

They soon found out. Nanny Piggins produced two marshmallows and snuffed them up her nose.

'Brilliant!' exclaimed Boris. 'She's blocking the smell of the cake.'

Nanny Piggins ran on, widening the gap between her and the rest of the field. She made it to the tip in record time before turning around and heading back to town. From there on, the only thing that slowed her down was stopping to blow a raspberry at Nanny Anne as she passed her going the other way, and telling off the volunteers at the drinks station for only providing water and no chocolate milk.

In a few short minutes Nanny Piggins was running back into central Dulsford.

'Here she comes!' cried Samantha as they spotted Nanny Piggins at the far end of the High Street on the last straight stretch into town.

The crowd burst into cheers and applause.

'She's going to win!' exclaimed Boris delightedly.

'She's going to win by a mile!' said Derrick.

Indeed, it was only as Nanny Piggins sprinted

down the last hundred metres that they saw Nanny Anne appear in the distance at the far end of the street.

'You can do it, Nanny Piggins!' cried Samantha.

The official announcer's voice crackled over the public address system: 'And here comes Sarah Matahari Lorelai Piggins in the lead.'

The crowd roared their approval.

'It is the first time we've had a woman, and a pig, come in first place,' continued the announcer. 'What a wonderful tribute to the power of exercise and healthy living.'

At that exact moment Nanny Piggins' legs stopped and she skidded to a halt just five metres short of the line.

'Did he just say I was a tribute to the power of exercise and healthy living?' asked Nanny Piggins.

'Yes,' said Derrick.

'That's the whole point,' urged Tyler. 'To win over the healthy vote.'

'I can't do it,' said Nanny Piggins.

'Yes you can!' yelled Tyler. 'You just need to take a few more steps.'

'Nanny Anne is getting closer,' cried Samantha.

'I can't win this race,' said Nanny Piggins as though awaking from a stupor. 'To do so would betray everything I believe in. I don't believe in unnecessary sweating, jogging or organised sport in any of its forms. I certainly don't believe in role models, health messages or setting a good example.'

'But you'll never become mayor on that platform,' wailed Tyler.

'I don't care. Some things are more important than politics,' declared Nanny Piggins. 'Like principles and beliefs. And I believe in cake, fun and more cake!'

The crowd roared their approval, then swept forward and lifted Nanny Piggins onto their shoulders, chanting 'We want Piggins! We want Piggins!'

Nanny Piggins was carried over to the winner's podium where she took the microphone and broke into an impromptu loser's acceptance speech.

'I am Nanny Piggins and I am running for mayor,' declared Nanny Piggins, 'but I will not go against my principles by jogging to do so.'

'She did run 9.995 kilometres of the 10 km run,' whispered Derrick.

'A slight technicality,' dismissed Boris.

'In fact,' continued Nanny Piggins, 'the only reason I am here today is because I was tricked by my campaign advisor.' Nanny Piggins pointed dramatically at Tyler.

'I didn't trick you,' said Tyler. 'I persuaded you using reasoned argument and polling data.'

'The most dangerous type of political trick of all,' condemned Nanny Piggins, 'which leads me to wonder, why would a self-proclaimed "professional campaign strategist" try to lure me into a life of deceit and lies?'

'You're talking about jogging, innocent jogging,' protested Tyler.

'There is nothing innocent about that much sweating and bouncing up and down,' condemned Nanny Piggins. 'You have systematically made me turn my back on everything I believe in. And I know of only one political mastermind morally bankrupt enough to do that – my identical twin sister, Abigail!'

Everyone in the crowd gasped.

Tyler (aka Abigail) tried to make a run for it but unfortunately she slammed into Nanny Anne just as she crossed the line. So Abigail fell over and her wig and glasses fell off, revealing herself to be an exact replica of Nanny Piggins (except that she had long red hair and green eyes).

The crowd gasped again.

'This is as good as *The Young and the Irritable*,' whispered Boris. 'I wish I'd brought a bowl of popcorn.'

'Yes, it's me,' admitted Abigail (formerly known as Tyler), 'but you had it coming. Remember when we were children and you borrowed my pink cardigan without asking, then got a toffee stain all down the front. I told you I'd get you back and now I have.'

'But that cardigan didn't suit you at all,' argued Nanny Piggins. 'It clashed with your hair.'

'That's not the point!' yelled Abigail. 'It's the principle of the matter.'

'You see, everyone,' said Nanny Piggins. 'This is how dangerous principles are. It allows one impossibly beautiful pig to carry a grudge against another impossibly beautiful pig for all these years. Which is why, if you elect me mayor, I promise to be unprincipled at all times.'

The crowd cheered again.

'What about my medal?' panted Nanny Anne.

'You can have it,' said Nanny Piggins, handing the large winner's gold medal to her, 'although I don't see how you can enjoy it. It's not made of chocolate at all. I know because I bit it to be sure.'

Nanny Anne took the medal, then collapsed under the weight of it due to inadequate carbo-loading.

'Only one question remains,' continued Nanny Piggins. 'Why? Abigail is usually in far flung, not terribly democratic countries influencing national elections one way or another. Why would she come to a small town like Dulsford and get involved with a mayoral election?'

'I told you,' sulked Abigail. 'The pink cardigan.'

'That might have been part of it, but there had to be more,' said Nanny Piggins. 'How did you find out? Who got in touch with you?'

'I don't know what you're talking about,' lied Abigail.

'Then perhaps you do – Mr Green!' accused Nanny Piggins, dramatically pointing at him.

Mr Green flinched, then looked scared as the whole crowd turned and glared at him.

'It wasn't me. I didn't do anything. You can't prove it,' he babbled.

'Do I have to come down there and stomp on your foot?' asked Nanny Piggins.

Mr Green's shoulders slumped. 'All right, everything she says is true.'

'I knew it!' declared Nanny Piggins.

Nanny Piggins spent the rest of the afternoon shaking hands, signing autographs and refusing to kiss babies (they are terribly unhygienic) for the crowd.

When they finally made it home she certainly

needed the tall glass of chocolate milk that Boris poured for her.

'What a day,' said Nanny Piggins.

'Are you hurt that your sister turned up and tried to ruin your fledging political career?' asked Derrick.

'Of course not,' said Nanny Piggins. 'I'd be hurt if she hadn't. It's always nice to know that family cares. Even if they only care about thwarting you.'

'Are you cross with Father?' asked Samantha.

'A little,' admitted Nanny Piggins, 'but I'll forgive him as soon as I shake a bag of itching powder into his underpants drawer. Then it will be like this whole incident never happened.'

'So, no jogging for you?' asked Michael.

'Goodness no!' said Nanny Piggins. 'I've promised the organisers I'll enter again next year.'

'You have?!' exclaimed the children.

'Yes, but only if they adopt my brilliant suggestion,' said Nanny Piggins. 'I told them to run the race from the town to the cake factory. If the cake factory is the finish line, everyone will run much faster. They're going to call it "The Cake Run".'

## CHAPTER 3

### *Colonel Troubles*

Nanny Piggins was standing in the living room, posing for her mayoral statue. I know this seems a little presumptuous (the election was still a month away) and extremely egotistical (she was way behind in the polls). But it was traditional for the newly elected mayor of Dulsford to commission a portrait of himself or, in this case, herself. And if Nanny Piggins got elected she had no intention of doing anything dull. She wanted to have an enormous statue of herself made entirely out of marzipan. That way it would be a piece of art the people of Dulsford could actually enjoy, by licking the sugary almondy goodness every time they walked past it.

Fortunately Nanny Piggins was dear friends with the world's leading marzipan artist, Piers Flom of Belgium. And he was delighted to fly in and craft a masterpiece for her, in exchange for six tea chests full of her chocolate fudge brownies. (Like Nanny Piggins, he preferred to make financial transactions in cake. Cash can lose its value but cake has an inherent undisputable worth.) Piers only had a brief window of availability before he had to fly to South America and craft a 60-metre-high statue of an up-and-coming dictator, so this was why Nanny Piggins was forced to pose for this pre-emptive statue. She reasoned it was worth doing because even if she lost, she could always put it in the front garden and invite local children to come over and lick it instead.

Nanny Piggins was just entering the third hour of holding her pose (she had chosen to pose holding a cake in the air in triumph) when there was a knock at the door.

'Who could that be?' asked Nanny Piggins.

'*Je ne sais pas*,' said Piers, which is Belgian for 'I haven't the foggiest'.

'There's no way Mirabella could have discovered you're here, is there?' asked Nanny Piggins, growing alarmed.

Mirabella Coeur was the world's second greatest marzipan artist. She and Piers had a fierce rivalry. They would often turn up at each other's events and denounce each other, partly because Mirabella believed in a modern expressionist style of marzipan art whereas Piers was a conservative practitioner of traditional marzipan values. But mainly because, of course, they were secretly in love with each other but had not realised it yet.

'If it is her, let her in,' said Piers. 'I am not afraid of that woman.' A statement he truly believed, even though he unconsciously contradicted himself by slipping a paint palette into the seat of his pants in case she burst in and started kicking him.

'I'll go and see,' said Michael. He was eager to answer the door because he had never seen two confectioners fight before.

But it was not to be.

'It's the retired Army Colonel who lives round the corner,' said Michael. 'He wants to know if he can come in and talk to you.'

Nanny Piggins sighed. 'If he has come round to propose to me again, I don't have time for it today.

Tell him to come back on the weekend. Then I can bake him his favourite Dundee cake, which should soften the blow when I refuse.'

'I don't think he's come to propose today,' said Michael. 'He's brought a friend who's wearing a military uniform with a very smart hat, and his leg is in a cast.'

'Has *he* come round to propose?' asked Nanny Piggins, suspiciously. She intensely disliked being proposed to by men she had not even met.

'They say they have a problem they want your help with,' said Michael.

'What do you think, Piers?' asked Nanny Piggins. 'Have I been posing long enough? Will you be able to continue without me for a while?'

'Oui, oui,' said Piers. 'If you leave your shoes I can focus on your feet until you return.'

And so Nanny Piggins, still wearing her mayoral robes (homemade from red crepe paper, cotton balls for the fur trim, and linked chocolate coins for the mayoral necklace), led her impromptu guests into the kitchen where she got out a cake and a pot of tea. (Military men always like tea.)

After the Colonel's friend had finished saying, 'Mmmm-mmm-mmm, this is sooooo delicious,' many times (he had never tried one of Nanny Piggins' cakes before), they got down to business.

'What seems to be the problem?' asked Nanny Piggins.

'Well, Bert here was my sergeant in the –' began the Colonel. 'Actually, I can't tell you which campaigns because it is all top-secret and hush-hush. But we fought side by side in many a sticky situation.'

'Oh I know all about sticky situations,' sympathised Nanny Piggins. 'I once fell in a vat of maple syrup. Fortunately I had a large supply of pancakes on hand so I was able to eat my way out.'

'Yes,' agreed the Colonel, 'well anyway, Bert is a good chap. But he is a Drill Sergeant now, in charge of training troops for the elite bombardiers squad.'

'I know them!' said Nanny Piggins, surprising the Colonel because generally Nanny Piggins was not well versed on anything to do with the military. (She thought his medals were a collection of rare chocolate coins he had picked up on his travels.) 'The bombardiers are the ones who wear those jaunty brown berets, aren't they?'

'Yes, actually they are,' said Bert the Drill Sergeant. 'Only men who have completed the arduous training program have the privilege of wearing the brown beret.'

'More accessories should come with arduous requirements,' said Nanny Piggins. 'If men were required to do fifty jumping jacks before they put on a fedora, perhaps the extra oxygen flow to their brain would make them realise how silly they looked.'

'Anyway, the problem is,' continued the Drill Sergeant, deciding it was better not to try to follow Nanny Piggins' logic, 'we are not getting the quality of recruits we used to get.'

'What do you mean?' asked Nanny Piggins.

'It's young people today,' explained the Colonel. 'They're all wishy-washy.'

'They are?' asked Nanny Piggins.

'To be strictly fair,' said the Drill Sergeant, 'I have been a Drill Sergeant for twenty years now and in that time the recruits have always been wishy-washy.'

'I suppose that young people with lots of initiative and enthusiasm prefer to go into more active fields, like confectionary research and ice-cream making,' guessed Nanny Piggins. 'The military would be too dull for them.'

'The problem is that the rules have changed,' explained the Drill Sergeant. 'We're not allowed to do any of the things we used to do to motivate the raw young recruits.'

'What sort of things did you used to do?' asked Nanny Piggins.

'Make them stand in the rain, force them to do push-ups and yell mean names at them right in their faces,' said the Drill Sergeant.

'I see,' said Nanny Piggins. 'That doesn't sound terribly pleasant.'

'But if you don't yell at them they don't do as they're told,' complained the Drill Sergeant. 'Last week when I told them to clean the latrines (army-speak for toilets) with their toothbrushes, they all ran away and hid behind the mess hall (army-speak for dining room).'

'That shows good evasive instincts,' approved Nanny Piggins. 'Heading for the nearest source of food.'

'Yes, but when I chased after them,' said the Drill Sergeant, 'I slipped over on a potato and tore my Achilles tendon.'

'Vegetables cause so much pain,' said Nanny Piggins sadly, shaking her head. 'So why have you come to me for help?'

'Because the army needs troops with bravery, gusto, athleticism, strategic thinking and an appetite for violence,' explained the Colonel. 'Which made me think of you.'

'Why, Colonel,' said Nanny Piggins, 'I think that is the most romantic thing you have ever said to me.' For the first time since they had known each other the Colonel had made Nanny Piggins blush.

'We were hoping you could join my unit, fill in for me as a temporary Drill Sergeant and lead the troops by example,' said the Drill Sergeant. 'They've got important war games coming up in two weeks. I don't mind if they don't win, but I don't want them to embarrass me in front of the other Drill Sergeants.'

'Go on, say you'll do it,' pleaded the Colonel. 'Show them how a warrior should behave.'

'I don't know,' said Nanny Piggins. 'I am tremendously busy. I'm running for mayor and I was planning to roast marshmallows this afternoon.'

'But this will help your mayoral campaign!' exclaimed the Colonel. 'Voters love a candidate with a military track record.'

'Really?' asked Nanny Piggins.

'It might help them overlook your criminal record,' suggested Derrick.

'I don't know,' said Nanny Piggins. 'Posing as a Drill Sergeant does sound fun, but I already have a full schedule posing for a giant marzipan statue.'

'We'll make it worth your while,' said the Colonel.

'How?' asked Nanny Piggins.

The Colonel nodded at the Drill Sergeant meaningfully.

'We'll buy you a chocolate cake,' said the Drill Sergeant. He'd clearly been coached in what to say.

'Deal!' exclaimed Nanny Piggins, leaping to her feet and shaking both men by the hand. 'I was worried for a moment you were going to offer me a medal, which would have been a tremendous honour, but I couldn't have accepted it. I wouldn't have liked to pin anything through my dress because it's silk, you see.'

'So will you come with me right away?' asked the Drill Sergeant.

'Of course,' said Nanny Piggins. 'I'll just use the photocopier in Mr Green's office to make a photocopy of my face. That will give Piers a good visual reference to be going on with. Then I'm all yours.'

'You lucky man,' sighed the Colonel.

'But what about us?' said Derrick.

'Who will look after us if you go off and join the army?' asked Samantha.

'You're coming with me,' said Nanny Piggins, surprised that they had ever thought otherwise. 'You'll be my assistants.'

'The army doesn't normally allow under-age recruits,' said the Drill Sergeant.

'Pish,' said Nanny Piggins. 'We'll just lie about their age and say they are unnaturally short due to chocolate deficiency in their diet when they were babies. If anyone questions it we'll accuse them of discrimination against the chocolate deprived.'

And so Nanny Piggins and the children got in the Drill Sergeant's jeep and were driven off to a remote training base deep in the forest. The base consisted of several long corrugated iron barracks, a parade ground, a shooting range and lots of tricky obstacle courses, and exercise equipment for training fit young men to become even fitter young men, with a total disregard for their own safety. When the jeep pulled up the raw recruits were lined up ready for Nanny Piggins to inspect them. They were an intimidating sight: twelve athletic young men, all immaculately dressed in khaki and standing at attention. They did not look wishy-washy with their buzz cuts and obvious brawn.

'What do I do first?' whispered Nanny Piggins to the Drill Sergeant.

'Traditionally,' said the Drill Sergeant, 'a Drill Sergeant starts out by saying lots of mean things about how the men are useless good-for-nothings. Then you go along and give each of them a horrible nickname.'

'Why?' asked Nanny Piggins.

'There are twelve of them,' said the Drill Sergeant. 'It's hard remembering all their real names.'

'All right,' said Nanny Piggins, 'I think I can handle that.'

She stepped forward and looked the first man up and down, then walked along the line, tapping each soldier on the chest as she renamed him. 'Victor, Bridge, Crevasse, Michelangelo, Reef, Thunder, Vincent, Hadrian, Vincello, Tub, Peregrine and Thor – they are your new nicknames.'

Nanny Piggins walked back to where the children were standing.

'But they're all names of characters from *The Young and the Irritable*,' whispered Derrick.

'I know,' said Nanny Piggins. 'I thought it would give them some inspiring role models to live up to.'

Nanny Piggins turned to face the men, using her fiercest glower. 'I understand that you have all been very naughty boys,' said Nanny Piggins. 'You have been ignoring your Drill Sergeant.'

Several of the soldiers sniggered.

'You think it's funny to ignore a man who has dedicated his life to training soldiers so that they don't get blown up in battle?' snapped Nanny Piggins.

'No, I think it's funny that you called us naughty boys,' said Vincello.

Now all the other soldiers sniggered.

'Are you laughing at me?' asked Nanny Piggins.

'Yes,' laughed Vincello.

'Right,' said Nanny Piggins. 'Do any of you think you can run faster than me?'

The men laughed again. 'Of course we do,' said Vincello. 'You're only four feet tall.'

'And you're wearing a dress,' added Peregrine.

'I suspected that would be your attitude,' said Nanny Piggins. She turned to the children. 'Michael, please produce the cake I made earlier.'

'Yes, Nanny Piggins,' said Michael as he obediently opened her expansive handbag and produced a beautiful chocolate mud cake, so sweet and sticky that it glistened in the sun.

A gentle wind blew across the parade ground and wafted the smell of the heavenly cake in the direction of the men.

Several of the men groaned with longing, some even said, 'Cawww, look at that!'

'This cake is the reward for the first man to catch me,' said Nanny Piggins.

'So we have to chase you, and if we catch you, you'll give us that cake?' clarified Vincello.

'That's right,' confirmed Nanny Piggins.

'When do we start?' asked Thor.

'Look over there!' exclaimed Nanny Piggins. 'The General is giving away free computer games!'

The men turned to look and when they turned back Nanny Piggins was sprinting down the road carrying the cake.

The men realised they had been tricked and ran after her. And that is how Nanny Piggins enticed the men into doing their first 30 mile route march. They chased her all day and into the night, not realising that Nanny Piggins had actually hidden up a tree as soon as she was out of sight, eaten the cake herself and gone back to the base for a lie down and a game of cards with the children.

At eight o'clock that night, she took pity on the men and drove out in a truck to fetch them.

'So where's our cake?' asked Vincello. (He was too exhausted to snigger now.)

'I ate it,' said Nanny Piggins truthfully. 'I knew you wouldn't catch me.'

'Awww, that's not fair,' complained Bridge. (He particularly liked cake.)

'All's fair in love and cake,' said Nanny Piggins.

'I think the expression is "All's fair in love and war",' corrected Crevasse. (He was a bookish soldier.)

'That may be what humans say,' said Nanny Piggins, 'but we pigs say "all's fair in love and cake" because cake baking is much more brutal and cut-throat than any war. Now come along, back to the barracks. I'll have another exercise for you tomorrow and you can have another chance to get a cake then.'

The next morning the men were awoken by Nanny Piggins standing in the middle of the barracks, banging a ladle on a saucepan. 'Wake up, wake up,' she ordered.

'What's going on?' asked Thor.

'Today you are going to learn rope climbing,' declared Nanny Piggins.

'Stuff that, I'm going back to bed,' said Vincello.

'Very well,' said Nanny Piggins, 'but first you might like to have a look at this. Samantha, show them today's cake.'

Samantha opened a cake box to reveal a beautiful caramel glacé angel cake. A cake so good it smelt like it had descended from heaven. It was fresh out of the oven, and the only thing that smells better than cake is warm cake. And the only thing that smells better than warm cake is warm cake covered in runny caramel glacé.

The men all got out of bed and some even started lunging for the cake (for which we must not judge them too harshly. They had missed their dinner the night before and were yet to have their breakfast. So they were practically delirious with cake longing). Luckily Boris was on hand to act as bodyguard to the cake.

'A-a-ah,' warned Boris, standing between the men and the cake. 'Now, unlike my sister I do not believe in violence. But I do believe in sitting on people who don't do as they are told, and I am a little bigger-boned than the average human –' This was Boris' way of saying he weighed 700 kilograms – 'so if I sat on you, you might not find it comfortable.'

'The only way you're getting that cake,' said Nanny Piggins, 'is by doing as you're told.'

The men were soon out on the training ground, standing beneath a 15 metre rope.

'We can't climb that, it's too high,' complained Peregrine.

'You don't have to climb it,' said Nanny Piggins. 'You are welcome to stay here on the ground if you like. But I have stationed Derrick and the cake on the platform at the top.'

Derrick leaned over the edge of the platform and waved a slice of cake.

'So if you want some cake you'd better get up there,' said Nanny Piggins.

The men all rushed forward and fought over who was going to get first go, which actually gave them all a good, practical, half-hour lesson in hand-to-hand combat training before the first soldier even had a go.

Eventually, Peregrine, who had a particular knack for noogies, won out, took hold of the rope and started climbing. Now, climbing a rope is very difficult under the best of conditions. The rope wiggles, your arms get achy and the skin on your fingers gets terribly roughed up. It's hard to hold on, let alone climb upwards. But it just so happens that Nanny Piggins had made it especially difficult by smearing golden syrup all over the rope. True, the syrup did make the rope sticky, which helped a little. But it also made the rope slimy, which did not help at all. Plus, the syrup made the rope very attractive to bees. So Peregrine was only a metre off the ground when a bee started buzzing around his head. He panicked, let go and landed on his bottom.

The other men surged forward to have a try, and try they did, all morning, but not one of them got further than a couple of metres off the ground.

'This is ridiculous,' complained Vincello. 'It's impossible. No-one can climb that.'

'Really?' said Nanny Piggins. 'Then watch this.'

Nanny Piggins grabbed the rope and climbed up it so quickly it was as though she had a jet pack installed under her dress. (She did not, she was just good at climbing rope.) Soon she was standing on the platform looking down at the soldiers.

'And now,' announced Nanny Piggins, 'I am going to eat the cake.'

'But you promised that to us,' complained Thor.

'Don't worry,' said Nanny Piggins. 'I shall eat it very slowly. If you get up here quickly enough, I shall share it with you.'

The men launched into action.

'We'll never get up there individually,' said Vincello. 'Our hands are all too sore. And Crevasse's head has swollen up from being stung by a bee. The only way we'll get up there is if we work as a team and form a human pyramid.'

And that is what they did. They organised themselves into rows, climbed up on each other's shoulders, building a higher and higher structure with their own bodies until Thunder (the smallest and lightest soldier) was able to grab hold of the platform and pull himself up by his fingertips, just in time to see Nanny Piggins pop the last slice of cake in her mouth.

'Well done,' she said with a muffled voice because her mouth was so full of cake. 'Excellent teamwork. You're improving.'

And so the training regimen continued. Every morning Nanny Piggins would force the soldiers out of bed with another brutal training exercise, fuelled by the promise of cake if they succeeded. She got them crawling underneath barbed wire by dragging cupcakes on strings in front of them; scaling cliff faces by throwing Madeira cake off first; and she got them running the obstacle course in record time by sticky-taping an exploding coffee cake to the top of the last obstacle.

But on Friday morning things did not go so smoothly. Nanny Piggins entered the barracks banging her saucepan at 4 am, but none of the men got out of bed. They did not even look up.

'Go away,' said Vincello.

'Perhaps you've overtired them,' worried Boris.

'Perhaps,' agreed Nanny Piggins, 'but we'll soon fix that. Today I'm strapping a sticky date pudding to the underside of a remote control aeroplane to see if you can catch it. I thought we could go and do it in the forest, so you get lots of practice climbing trees, hiding behind branches, and leaping out at things that are flying past.'

'We're not interested,' said Peregrine.

'Really?' said Nanny Piggins. She turned to the children and Boris. 'I'm not losing my touch, am I? This sticky date pudding smells seriously good to me.'

Boris sniffed it. 'It's definitely seriously good. It's taking all my willpower not to lick it.'

'I saw you lick it on the walk over here,' said Michael.

'I know,' said Boris, 'which makes it even harder to resist licking it again.'

'We don't need your sticky date pudding or your cake or your desserts,' said Thor. 'We've got our own.'

'What are you talking about?' asked Nanny Piggins. 'Have you learnt to be bakers? If so I must congratulate you. I will happily help you run away from the army so you can pursue a much more important career in baked goods.'

'No, we just rang a bakery and got them to deliver all the types of cakes you've been tormenting us with,' said Vincello, 'then we sat up all night eating. We couldn't eat another thing if we wanted to.'

'But where did you get the cake from?' asked Nanny Piggins.

'A local place,' said Thunder. 'What was it called?'

'I've got their business card,' said Vincello. 'It was Hans' Bakery.'

Nanny Piggins gasped. 'The treachery! How could Hans do that to me?'

'To be fair,' said Samantha, 'Hans didn't know that you were secretly training an elite military unit in the woods.'

'No, but he could have guessed,' said Nanny Piggins. 'Remind me to have a stern word with him when I see him next.'

'Can you go now?' asked Crevasse. 'We'd like to have a lie-in.'

'But the war games are in five days and you're not ready!' protested Nanny Piggins.

'Are you kidding?!' complained Vincello. 'In the last week you've had us climb ropes, hike mountains, master taekwondo, crawl through mud, swim through a swamp and learn all the words and harmonies to *HMS Pinafore*. We're the most thoroughly trained soldiers in the country.'

'Yes, you know all the military techniques and the Gilbert and Sullivan harmonies,' agreed Nanny Piggins, 'but you don't have the killer instincts.'

'The Drill Sergeant said you're not actually allowed to kill anybody,' warned Derrick.

'No, I mean the absolute determination to succeed at any cost,' said Nanny Piggins. 'Training is good, but an untrained enemy who is truly determined will beat skilled soldiers every time.'

'You're talking rubbish,' said Peregrine.

'I'll prove it to you,' said Nanny Piggins, 'with one more training exercise.'

All the men groaned.

'It will be a simple one,' said Nanny Piggins. 'You will just have to defend the sweet shop in town.'

'From who?' asked Thunder.

'All the neighbourhood children,' said Nanny Piggins, 'and one or two sweet-loving adults.'

The men laughed.

'Sounds like a piece of cake,' said Bridge.

'That expression has always baffled me,' said Nanny Piggins, shaking her head. 'There is nothing easy about a piece of cake. It certainly isn't easy to make one properly. People are forever making terrible mistakes such as putting carrot in it or using low fat spread instead of butter.'

'What happens if we do this?' asked Vincello.

'If you succeed,' said Nanny Piggins, 'and defend the sweet shop so not one sweet, lolly or chocolate is eaten between six and twelve on Saturday morning, I will go away and leave you all alone.'

'Hurray!' cheered the men.

'But,' said Nanny Piggins, 'if I win, you have to do fifty push-ups, compose an opera about me and how I'm always right, bake me an enormous chocolate cake and always do everything the Drill Sergeant says from now on.'

The men conferred, mumbling among themselves.

'What equipment can we use to defend this sweet shop?' asked Vincello.

'Any military equipment you like,' said Nanny Piggins. 'Just no guns or explosives. The mothers wouldn't like that. They are reluctant enough to let their children come over to our house for a play date as it is.'

The soldiers looked at each other and nodded. They were in agreement.

'You're on,' said Vincello.

83

The morning of what in future years would be known as *The Battle of the Dulsford Sweet Shop* dawned. The soldiers had set up a large reinforced barricade on one side of the sweet shop, and to defend the other side (because it was a corner shop and therefore vulnerable on two fronts), they had parked an enormous tank.

'Tsk, tsk, tsk,' said Nanny Piggins.

She, Boris and the children were hiding in the bushes of a garden opposite, using binoculars to watch everything the soldiers did. 'Those naughty boys. I told them no guns.'

'I guess they think a tank is okay if they don't actually fire it, they just use it as a blockade,' said Derrick.

'I'm impressed by their deviousness,' said Nanny Piggins. 'Perhaps they learnt more from me than I realised.'

'Do you still think we can win?' asked Samantha.

'Oh yes,' said Nanny Piggins. 'I have plenty of tricks up my sleeve.' Nanny Piggins glanced at her watch. 'In fact, it's time to deploy our first weapon.' Nanny Piggins took out a walkie-talkie and spoke into it. 'Cue the first assault.'

'Are you going to use a cannon?' asked Michael hopefully.

'No, something much more dangerous,' said Nanny Piggins. 'Here she comes.'

The children peered through the bushes and saw the distinctive perfect blonde curls of seven-year-old Margaret Wallace as she rode her tricycle down the street. She looked so sweet and innocent in her perfectly ironed pink frilly dress and pigtails. Margaret stopped right by the barricade.

'Go away, little girl,' hissed Vincello from behind the barricade. 'This is a military training exercise.'

Then Margaret Wallace did the unthinkable. She burst into tears. 'I want my mummy!' wailed Margaret, with startling volume for such a diminutive child.

'Shhhh, shush,' pleaded the soldiers. 'We can't help you, we're busy.'

'I want my mummmmmmy!' wailed Margaret, even louder.

Nanny and the children could hear the soldiers arguing among themselves. Eventually Vincello stuck his head out from behind the barricade, looked both ways to see if the coast was clear, then ran out to Margaret Wallace and gave her a hug.

Nanny Piggins nodded approvingly. 'I knew Vincello was leadership material.'

'It's all right,' said Vincello. 'If you come in the shop we can call your mummy from there.'

As he picked Margaret up and turned back to the shop, Margaret's face was turned to where Nanny Piggins was hiding. Margaret gave a big wink.

'She's in,' said Nanny Piggins triumphantly.

They watched Vincello carry Margaret back to the shop, and as soon as he unlocked the front door, Nanny Piggins stood up, whipped a bugle out of her handbag and blasted a resounding signal.

Two hundred neighbourhood children simultaneously jumped out from their hiding spots all around the sweet shop. Unlike the unimaginative soldiers, the children had thought to attack on all six sides (left, right, front, back, the rooftops and below, through the cellar via the green grocer next door). They all ran, leapt and launched themselves at the sweet shop among the deafening sound of cheers, whoops and shrieks of delight.

'That's awesome,' said Derrick, 'but surely the soldiers will be able to hold them off. They're just children.'

'I have another secret weapon,' said Nanny Piggins. She took out the walkie-talkie again. 'Melanie, you're up.'

In an instant Melanie, the fat lady from the circus, burst out of her hiding place – the telephone booth across the street. (It is amazing that she ever fit in there, but at the circus she had learnt a thing or two from the clowns who jam themselves into the tiny car.) When the children had last seen her, Melanie weighed an impressive 400 kilograms, but she had been working at her craft since then and now easily weighed 450 kilograms. As she ran at the barricade at full speed, wobbling and screaming 'CHOCOLATE!', she was an astonishing sight.

The local children had all been forewarned, so they all got out of the way. But the soldiers had never expected to be charged by a huge bellowing fat lady – they had no idea what to do. She ran right over the top of them, slammed into the front door of the shop and knocked it right off its hinges. The children streamed inside, grabbing sweets off the shelves and shoving them in their mouths.

'Now for the piece of resistance,' said Nanny Piggins as she got up and pulled back a bush to reveal her old cannon from the circus.

'How long has that been there?' marvelled Derrick.

'I had it installed months ago,' said Nanny Piggins. 'I thought it important to have artillery on hand in case trouble broke out and the sweet shop needed to be defended.'

'But you're going to use it to *attack* the sweet shop,' said Samantha.

'I know,' agreed Nanny Piggins. 'It's funny how these things work out so conveniently.'

Nanny Piggins climbed into her cannon, Boris lit the fuse and Nanny Piggins blasted out across the street yelling, 'IIIIIII TOOOOOOLLLLLD YOOOOOOOUUUU SOOOOOOO!' as she flew over the heads of the bamboozled soldiers, smashed through the upstairs window of the shop and ran downstairs to join in all the fun.

'Shall we join them?' asked Boris, holding out his hand to Derrick, Samantha and Michael. 'I'll help you get past the soldiers. I'll roar at them and pretend to be fierce if they give you any trouble.'

'Forget that,' said Michael. 'I'll roar at them and pretend to be fierce myself.' He leapt out and ran towards the shop; Derrick soon followed and even Samantha, who was usually so trepidatious, had a rush of blood to the head (perhaps inspired by the heady scent of confectionery in the air) and took off towards the sweet shop with Boris jogging behind.

A few short minutes later, two hundred exhausted children sat outside on the footpath finishing off the last of the sweets. The soldiers nursed their wounds, which were mainly psychological, although there was one hard-boiled-lolly-to-the-eye injury, a candy cane up the nose to remove and a victim of a particularly nasty wedgie. (He had been standing in front of the fudge counter, so he only had himself to blame.)

Nanny Piggins sat on the gutter, proudly licking the last of the chocolate off her trotters with a very smug expression on her face.

The Colonel and his friend the Drill Sergeant pulled up in their jeep.

'Drill Sergeant, how wonderful to see you!' said Nanny Piggins. 'I've broken the will of your men for you, and given them a short sharp lesson in military tactics.'

'All I've learnt is that children can be terrifying,' grumbled Peregrine.

'That's because they were properly motivated and focused on their objective,' said Nanny Piggins.

'They just wanted sweets,' complained Thor.

'Exactly,' said Nanny Piggins. 'If you can master that level of intensity and single purpose you will win any battle. Now that I have thoroughly thrashed you, I want you all to promise to do everything the Drill Sergeant says from now on.'

The men groaned.

'I know he can be mean and grumpy, and he wants you to do all sorts of wearisome exercises,' said Nanny Piggins, 'but he only does it because he loves you.'

'Steady on there,' said the Drill Sergeant. 'I wouldn't go that far.'

'You can hush up as well,' ordered Nanny Piggins.

'Yes ma'am,' said the Drill Sergeant.

'You might be so out of touch with your emotions that you don't realise how much you love your men,' said Nanny Piggins, 'but I can see it as clear as the slightly bent nose on your face. So I want you all to be good soldiers and do as the Drill Sergeant says. Otherwise I'll round up all these children, bring them down to the base and set them on you again.'

'We'll be good, we promise,' said the soldiers quickly.

'Remember you're not just doing this for yourselves or for your country,' said Nanny Piggins, 'you're doing it for the right to wear a jaunty little brown beret that will look fabulous on all of you.'

And so the men went back to the base having learnt a valuable lesson in military tactics – never take on a pig or two hundred hungry children.

Nanny Piggins, Boris, Derrick, Samantha and Michael went home for breakfast — the 20 metre tall statue of Nanny Piggins. They had to eat it because Mirabella had turned up before Piers had a chance to finish it, and she had vandalised the statue by sticking a huge marzipan moustache under Nanny Piggins' nose. Nanny Piggins thought it looked quite fetching, but she wanted to be mayor, not a bearded lady, plus she was peckish so she thought it best if they just ate the whole thing (she could always commission a chocolate statue to be carved later).

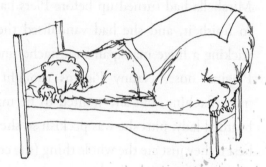

# CHAPTER 4

*Boris and the Big Snore*

Nanny Piggins, Boris and the children had enjoyed a busy morning. They had been paying a visit to the local fire station so that Boris could get his monthly shower. (When you are a ten-foot-tall bear with a serious honey habit, your fur does tend to become extremely matted.) And Boris was too tall to fit in a regular shower cubicle so when he needed a wash, Nanny Piggins took her brother to the fire station to be blasted with their giant hoses. It was very beneficial for the firemen as well, because Boris would run around screaming, 'Oooh aah oooh, it tickles, ooh stop it, oh more, that's the spot, again again again,' which was an excellent training exercise for them because it was just like having to put out a spreading bush fire.

But this was not the exhausting part of their morning. The exhausting part came after Nanny Piggins noticed that the firemen were throwing out their old pole, the one they used to use to get from their dormitory upstairs to the fire truck downstairs in super quick time.

The occupational health and safety officer had made them get rid of it because it was too likely to cause sprained ankles, completely ignoring the fact that sliding down a pole in the middle of the night with a siren blaring is so much fun it is totally worth any ankle injury.

Seeing the long brass pole lying there in the driveway, Nanny Piggins immediately knew she had to take it home. She was not quite sure what she would use it for but she knew anything that long and fun to slide down had a lot of potential.

Normally Nanny Piggins would have gone home, sat at the kitchen table and eaten cake as she contemplated the possibilities. But on this occasion it only took thinking of cake for Nanny Piggins to have a brilliant idea.

'I could run the pole from my bedroom down to the kitchen!' exclaimed Nanny Piggins. 'That way, if I fancy a slice of cake in the middle of the night there'll be no need to waste valuable time on opening the door or walking down the stairs in my hurry to get to it.'

So the next hour or two were spent chainsawing a hole in Nanny Piggins' bedroom floor. Followed by chainsawing another hole in Mr Green's bedroom floor when they realised he had the bedroom above the kitchen. (Nanny Piggins was not disappointed to have vandalised her own floor. She was sure there were advantages to having a hole in her room. For example, with the aid of a system of mirrors she would be able to watch *The Young and the Irritable* on the living room television without getting out of bed.)

All in all it was an action-packed morning. Especially for Boris whose job it was to stand in the kitchen, holding the pole in place while Nanny Piggins bolted the top to Mr Green's ceiling. It is always physically tiring work to hold something still for prolonged periods, but it is particularly wearisome when your overexcited sister keeps dropping her hammer onto your head from two floors above.

And it isn't as though Boris could let go of the pole to rub his head because then the pole would scoot away and Nanny Piggins would hit the floor, or even worse, the sore spot on Boris' head.

So Nanny Piggins was just painting olive oil on the pole (to make it extra slippery) before they all had a go, when disaster struck. Suddenly and unexpectedly the entire house began to shake, as a deafening rumble rattled the building from the foundations up.

'What's going on?' wailed Samantha.

'It must be an earthquake!' yelled Derrick.

'Either that, or someone in China has decided to dig a hole through the centre of the earth to come and visit us!' suggested Nanny Piggins.

Michael had a quick look out the window. 'I can't see any tunnels or tourists in the backyard!'

'Then we'd better take emergency evasive action!' decided Nanny Piggins.

'You mean, stand in a doorframe or take shelter under a desk?' asked Derrick.

'I was going to say "eat a slice of cake",' admitted Nanny Piggins. She had lived her entire life in a circus. And when your home is a tent, earthquakes are no great concern. If a large sheet of canvas or an aluminium pole falls on your head, you'll be fine. The greater concern is being a victim of cake looting during the aftermath. (Once there had been a cyclone that ravaged the circus and Nanny Piggins had been so busy providing first aid to her dear friend Esmeralda the elephant who had a speck of dust in her eye that she had not noticed when the fat lady snuck into her tent and ate her supply of mud cake.

Nanny Piggins did not hold it against Melanie. Eating is what fat ladies do, and if you are going to leave chocolate cake unguarded, that is tantamount to entrapment.)

At this point, the house was shaking so much that pictures started falling off the walls and furniture started vibrating away from their allocated floor spaces. 'Perhaps we better continue this discussion outside,' suggested Derrick.

'Good idea,' said Nanny Piggins as part of the ceiling collapsed on the floor next to her. 'If this is a terrible natural disaster we could dig up the emergency cake supplies I buried in the garden.'

Nanny Piggins decided that the quickest and safest way to get outside was to jump out the bedroom window. But having landed safely on the ground, she had difficultly persuading the children to follow her example. They had a much greater and more rational fear of head injuries than she did. So Nanny Piggins had to push over a wheelbarrow full of nice soft lawn clippings before they could escape the still trembling house. Samantha was so relieved to be safe on the ground that she gave Nanny Piggins an enormous hug, which was a good thing because it meant she did not notice when tiles started sliding off the roof and smashing onto the ground around her.

'Let's dig up the cake!' said Nanny Piggins excitedly. 'I remember I buried a particularly delicious marble cake near the maple tree.'

'Hang on,' said Michael, who was staring at the quivering house. 'Why is our house the only house in the street that's shaking?'

'It must be an extremely localised earthquake,' guessed Nanny Piggins.

'Perhaps it isn't an earthquake,' said Derrick.

'What are you saying?' asked Nanny Piggins. 'Do you think your father has rented out the space under the house to an evil scientist who is perfecting a doomsday device?'

But then something even more serious occurred to Samantha. 'Where's Boris?' she asked.

'He's usually the first person to run outside weeping when something unexpected happens,' said Michael, 'like being stung by a mosquito or not finding a toy in his box of honey puff breakfast cereal.'

'You don't think he's trapped inside under fallen debris, do you?' worried Samantha.

'He'll be all right,' Derrick assured her. 'He's used to being under fallen debris. The roof collapses on him all the time when he goes up to adjust the television aerial, then he gets inspired by the view, forgets where he is and launches into ballet.'

'I must go back inside and rescue him,' declared Nanny Piggins.

'But it's not safe,' said Samantha.

'Pish,' said Nanny Piggins. 'If I didn't do things just because they weren't safe, I'd never get out of bed in the morning.'

'Most people don't do quadruple twisting back-flips to get out of bed in the morning,' observed Michael.

'More fool them,' said Nanny Piggins. 'It's the best way to get to the rug without standing on the cold floorboards. Here, hold my chocolate bars. I'm going in.' Nanny Piggins pulled out the three dozen chocolate bars she had hidden about her person before marching purposefully towards the house.

'But what if the house collapses on top of you?' worried Samantha.

'I doubt it will,' said Nanny Piggins. 'Your father has done such a shoddy job of maintaining his property that I took it on myself to reinforce the framework by gaffer taping Mars Bars to all the load-bearing beams.'

'Why?' asked Derrick.

Nanny Piggins paused and thought about it for a moment. 'I'm not sure. It seemed like a good idea at the time. But then, perhaps that was because I was slightly delirious from eating so much chocolate. I had to test all the major chocolate bars to determine that the Mars Bar's combination of caramel to nougat offered the best tensile strength-to-weight ratio.'

Nanny Piggins disappeared in the house.

'I hope she'll be all right,' worried Samantha.

'I hope Boris is all right,' worried Michael.

'I hope Nanny Piggins accurately measured the tensile strength of Mars Bars and wasn't unconsciously swayed by their deliciousness,' worried Derrick.

But the children's concerns were allayed when, two seconds later, Nanny Piggins popped out the back door.

'Good news!' called Nanny Piggins. 'Boris is fine. And we aren't experiencing an extremely localised earthquake.'

'Then what is it?' asked Derrick.

'Boris has fallen into one of his super deep hibernation sleeps and is snoring,' explained Nanny Piggins.

'No way!' exclaimed Michael.

'Come and see for yourselves,' said Nanny Piggins.

A few minutes later, after they had donned their bicycle helmets for protection, Nanny Piggins and the children stood around the larder in the kitchen where Boris was lying fast asleep on the floor, with a smile on his face and a bucket of honey in his arms.

'The poor mite,' said Nanny Piggins affectionately. 'He was obviously tuckered out by all the home improvements we made this morning.'

'How are we going to wake him up?' asked Michael. 'Do you want me to fetch the fire extinguisher?'

'Or tip a huge bucket of ice over his head?' asked Samantha.

'Or whisper something controversial about ballet in his ear?' asked Derrick.

'No,' said Nanny Piggins, 'not this time. I know we usually wake Boris up when he falls into one of his hibernation sleeps, but on this occasion it is winter, and he has been getting crotchety lately.'

'He has?' asked Samantha.

'Oh yes,' said Nanny Piggins. 'Just last week I asked him to pass me the butter and he said, "No, get it yourself." And the week before that he forgot to say excuse me when he sneezed on Mrs Simpson.'

'And that's a bad sign?' asked Derrick.

'Oh yes,' said Nanny Piggins, 'When it's from a bear with such impeccable manners as Boris. No, he hasn't had a proper hibernation for years. He needs to have a good long rest. After all, he's a growing young bear.'

'But we can't leave him here in the house,' said Derrick. 'I don't care how many Mars Bars you've strapped to the framework, if he keeps this snoring up, it's going to bring the house down.'

'Also, I'm pretty sure this could be the turning point for Father,' said Michael. 'It's one thing not to notice a ten-foot-tall dancing bear living in the garden, but it's much harder not to notice a ten-foot-tall dancing bear who is snoring in your kitchen.'

'We'll just have to move Boris,' decided Nanny Piggins.

'How?' asked Samantha. 'He weighs –'

Nanny Piggins clamped her trotter over Samantha's mouth. 'Shhh. Just because he's asleep doesn't mean you can't hurt his feelings.'

'He weighs a little more than we could easily carry,' said Samantha, carefully wording the least offensive way of saying 700 kilograms.

'If the slaves could build the great pyramids of Egypt without cranes, bulldozers or anti-gravitational technology,' said Nanny Piggins, 'we must be able to shift one 700-kilogram bear.'

Boris jerked in his sleep, muttering, 'Big bones, not my fault.'

'Shhh,' said Derrick.

They were all quiet for a moment while Boris resettled.

'So how did the slaves build the great pyramids?' asked Michael.

'I'm not exactly sure,' admitted Nanny Piggins. 'I think it involved ropes, rolling logs and as much humus as they could eat.'

'Agghhh!' yelped Samantha as she noticed the clock.

'What's wrong?' asked Nanny Piggins.

'The time!' said Samantha.

'What's wrong with the time?' asked Nanny

Piggins. 'Do you think we should convert to a metric system. I'm not for it myself. If there were only ten hours in the day, when would I find time to eat cake?'

'Father is due home at two o'clock!' said Samantha.

'Why?' asked Nanny Piggins. 'He usually never gets home before midnight if he can avoid it.'

'A journalist from the local newspaper is meeting him here to do an interview about his mayoral campaign,' said Samantha.

'How typically aggravating of your father,' said Nanny Piggins. 'I know! Let's leave Boris here to sabotage your father's interview.'

'But that might sabotage Boris' life prospects,' said Derrick. 'What if Father panics and has him shipped back to Siberia?'

'Father panics when he sees a cockroach,' said Michael. 'I'm pretty sure he'll panic when he sees, and hears, a huge snoring bear . . . with a very petite figure,' added Michael hastily as Boris started to stir.

'Then we'd better get started,' declared Nanny Piggins. 'Michael, you go out to the shed and fetch some ropes. Derrick, you climb over the fence and chop down Mrs McGill's camphor laurel tree to turn it into logs. And Samantha, run down to the deli and get a big bucket of humus.'

'Really?' asked Samantha. 'Do you really think chickpea paste is essential?'

'There are crazy people out there who think aliens built the pyramids,' said Nanny Piggins. 'Is it any crazier to give the credit to humus?'

'Perhaps they didn't eat humus back then,' suggested Derrick. 'Perhaps apart from having prescient engineering technology, they were ahead of their time as bakers and they fed the slaves chocolate cake.'

'You're a genius!' exclaimed Nanny Piggins. 'That would explain so much. For example, why the Sphinx looks so smug. Because she had just eaten a mud cake!' Nanny Piggins turned to Samantha again. 'Go to Hans and get some cake instead. And quickly, we don't have much time.'

'What are *you* going to do?' asked Michael.

'Dress up as Cleopatra, of course,' said Nanny Piggins. 'If we are re-enacting the building techniques of ancient Egypt it would be a terrible shame to miss the opportunity to dress up as the most glamorous pig ever in history.'

'Cleopatra wasn't a pig,' said Samantha.

'Piffle!' exclaimed Nanny Piggins. 'You don't think a woman that glamorous, beautiful and politically powerful could have been a mere human, do you?'

When the children stopped and thought about it, it did make sense that Cleopatra was a distant relative of Nanny Piggins.

Fifteen minutes later, Boris was lying on top of a dozen rolling logs, and Nanny Piggins and the children were pulling him slowly across the yard using ropes tied round his legs.

'Heave!' encouraged Nanny Piggins.

They all heaved and Boris edged forward another centimetre.

'Gosh it's hard to move Boris,' said Michael as he dabbed the sweat from his brow.

'And that just goes to show what a great ballet dancer he is,' said Nanny Piggins. 'He moves himself about all the time, with comparatively little effort, and he makes it look so graceful.'

'We've still got seven metres to go,' said Samantha. 'We are moving him at a rate of about five centimetres per minute and Father is due home soon.'

'What's your point?' asked Nanny Piggins. (Maths was one of her few weaknesses.)

'We aren't going to get him in the shed in time,' said Samantha.

'There must be something we can do,' said Nanny Piggins. 'If only I had a cannon handy, I could blast him in there.'

'I know,' said Michael. 'The shed weighs less than Boris. Why don't we just pick up the shed and put it over him?'

'Brilliant!' declared Nanny Piggins.

'Do you think Father will notice that the shed is only half a metre from the back door?' asked Samantha.

'I doubt it,' said Nanny Piggins. 'He's unlikely to go outside. You know how your father claims the smell of grass gives him asthma.'

The children and Nanny Piggins soon placed the shed over the top of Boris, and it was an entirely successful method of hiding him from view. The only problem was that he could still be heard. (In fact, his snores could be heard several kilometres away in neighbouring towns.) And the shed was shaking with the vibrations.

'What are we going to do?' asked Derrick.

'We'll just have to soundproof the shed,' declared Nanny Piggins.

'How?' asked Samantha.

'I know!' said Michael. 'By blasting him into outer space!' He had heard somewhere that in space no-one could hear you scream, so he assumed no-one would be able to hear you snore either.

'Hmmm,' said Nanny Piggins, 'we could do

that. But from what he said, using very ungentlemanly language last time we spoke on the phone, I don't think the head of NASA is prepared to lend me the space shuttle again anytime soon. No, we'll just have to use egg cartons.'

'Egg cartons?' asked Samantha, suspecting her nanny of thinking of cake when she should be thinking of her brother.

'Yes,' said Nanny Piggins. 'Aside from protecting eggs, egg cartons have a wonderful ability to absorb sound. If you glue them to your walls it will soundproof a room.'

'But how many egg cartons would we need to line the walls of the shed?' asked Derrick.

'Well, the dimply half of an egg carton is thirty centimetres by ten centimetres. That means you would need thirty to fill one square metre. And Boris' shed is two metres by three metres by three metres, which is a surface area of 36 metres. So that would require 1080 egg cartons or, rather, 12,960 eggs, which, given that it takes four eggs to make a good sponge cake, equals 3240 cakes worth of eggs.' (Nanny Piggins was excellent at mathematics when it was applied to cake.)

'But we don't actually have to make that many cakes, do we?' asked Derrick.

'Of course we do,' said Nanny Piggins. 'If we are going to soundproof Boris' shed we can't leave 12,960 eggs rolling about on the floor. Your father might not notice a ten-foot-tall bear, but he would be sure to notice when he stood on one of the eggs and slipped over.'

The children imagined this scene and all secretly thought it would be worth trying, just to see their father lying on his back covered in raw egg yolk.

'But where are we going to get that many eggs from?' asked Samantha. 'I know you have friends who are chickens but do you know any chickens who have drivers' licences so they could bring their eggs here.'

'No need for that,' said Nanny Piggins. 'I know where we can get a large supply of eggs super quickly.' She took out the mobile phone she had 'borrowed' from Mr Green's pocket just that morning, and started dialling. 'I'm going to ask my friend the truck driver from the Slimbridge Cake Factory to help me out.' The phone started ringing. Then they heard the truck driver answer 'Hello' on the other end.

'Stan, darling, it's me,' said Nanny Piggins. 'I know it's Tuesday morning and you are usually driving the factory's weekly egg supply to the plant about now.'

'That's right,' agreed Stan.

'Oh good, then I hope you wouldn't mind terribly much if I hijack your entire truckload of eggs?' asked Nanny Piggins. 'I promise to wear a mask and be rough with you so that your bosses won't suspect a thing.'

(The management at the Slimbridge Cake Factory was well aware that it was Nanny Piggins who periodically hijacked their trucks, but she was such a good customer that they were prepared to turn a blind eye to it.)

'I don't know,' said Stan. 'I'm only a hundred metres from the front of the factory.'

'If you immediately make a U-turn and drive straight to our house, I'll make it worth your while,' said Nanny Piggins.

'You will?' said Stan hopefully. 'Will you give me a slice of your triple choc marble cake?'

'No,' said Nanny Piggins. 'I will give you an entire triple choc marble cake! Two if you get here in under three minutes.'

The children could hear the sound of the truck driver applying his compression brakes, skidding his truck through a 180-degree turn and working the engine up through the gears as he started speeding towards their house.

Nanny Piggins snapped the mobile phone shut. (Her favourite thing about 'borrowing' Mr Green's mobile was getting to make this dramatic gesture.)

'Excellent, everything is going to plan,' said Nanny Piggins. 'Now all we need to do is bake 3240 cakes, glue the egg cartons to the shed walls, then eat all the cakes before your father comes home, and he'll never know there is a hibernating bear hidden in his garden.'

'That sounds like a lot of work,' said Derrick.

'Ah, but the good thing about baking 3240 cakes is that if you start eating the first ones as soon as they come out of the oven, the sugary buttery goodness will give you the energy you need to power through the rest of the job,' explained Nanny Piggins. 'It's amazing what you can achieve with five or six hundred cakes in your stomach. This is why Henry VIII was such a successful king.'

And so, four and a half hours later, Nanny Piggins, the truck driver and the children were licking the cake crumbs from their fingers from the 3240th cake as they sat in the garden enjoying the peace and tranquillity of the now entirely sound-proofed shed.

Admittedly, you could still tell that Boris was in there snoring because the ground still vibrated with every intake of breath. But Mr Green would never notice that. He had not sat down on a patch of grass for 27 years because he so hated getting grass stains on his trousers, or to be strictly accurate, he hated paying drycleaners to get grass stains out of his trousers. In fact, when he proposed to Mrs Green he did it on a bitumen road because even though it was a lot more painful to go down on one knee, it saved him $5.60 in dry-cleaning fees.

At this moment the doorbell rang. (Mr Green had taken to ringing the doorbell even though it was his own house, because he did not want to walk in on Nanny Piggins and the children in the middle of one of their misdeeds. As a lawyer, he understood that the less he knew about their activities, the less he could be blamed for them in a court of law.)

'It's Father,' said Derrick.

'Should we hide?' asked Michael.

'Why?' asked Nanny Piggins.

'I don't know,' admitted Michael. 'It was just my first instinct.'

'Piggins, where are you?' bellowed Mr Green from inside the house.

Nanny Piggins sighed. 'I suppose I shouldn't bite him for yelling at me today, given the level of deceit we are trying to get past him. But your father's manners really are tiresome.'

'Ah, there you are,' said Mr Green as he opened the back door. Not that he could open it far, because the shed was so close to the wall. 'What are you doing? Nothing illegal, I hope?'

'Illegal? No,' said Nanny Piggins, which was strictly true. There was nothing illegal about hiding a Kodiak bear in a suburban backyard, although if the local council had imagined such a possibility, there surely would be.

'The journalist from the local paper will be here any minute,' said Mr Green through the narrow gap in the open doorway. 'I want you all to try to pretend to be normal for the duration of the visit. Do you understand?'

'Yes, Father,' chorused the children.

'I don't suppose I could persuade you to spend the duration quietly sitting in the cellar?' Mr Green asked Nanny Piggins.

'No,' said Nanny Piggins brightly.

'Not even for a chocolate cake?' asked Mr Green.

Nanny Piggins considered this for a nano-second. 'No, I'm all right,' said Nanny Piggins. 'I've had a fair amount of cake already today. But if you ask me again tomorrow, I'm sure I'd consider it.'

Fifteen minutes later the journalist showed up. From the glimpse of her shoes that Nanny Piggins could see under the crack in the door (through which they were spying on Mr Green), she could tell that the journalist was an intelligent sophisticated young woman of 28 and three-quarters. As such, it took the journalist all of four minutes to become bored with Mr Green's mundane answers to her questions and ask if she could have a look about the house. Mr Green tried to stop her but, unlike his nanny, he did not have a gift for fabricating spontaneous falsehoods. Plus women, especially young attractive ones, made him nervous.

So when she asked 'Why not?', Mr Green had to pause for several long moments before he came up with the answer. 'I don't have that information at this time,' said Mr Green. 'Could I get my secretary to send you my detailed response in letter form tomorrow?'

But it was too late. The journalist was already having a good stickybeak out the window.

'Why is your garden shed right up against your back door?' asked the journalist.

'It isn't,' said Mr Green, trying to block the journalist's view with his body. But even he was not stout enough for that.

'And why is there a pig and three children digging a hole in your garden?' asked the journalist.

'Would you believe that they were home intruders that I've never seen before in my life?' asked Mr Green.

'No,' said the journalist.

'Well then, the children are my children,' he reluctantly admitted.

'And the pig? Isn't she the pig who is running for mayor,' asked the journalist, a gleam appearing in her eye. Suddenly her story about Mr Green was becoming much more interesting. Instead of being hidden down the back of the paper it might appear in the front section, perhaps even on page two.

'She's an employee of mine,' hedged Mr Green.

'What does she do?' asked the journalist.

'I don't really know,' confessed Mr Green. 'That way, if she ever gets taken to court I can maintain plausible deniability.'

'No, I mean what does the pig do for you?' asked the journalist.

'She's my children's nanny,' confessed Mr Green.

'Really?' said the journalist. But this was a rhetorical question as she was too busy writing this all down to take in any more.

'You don't want to write about her,' said Mr Green. 'Nanny Piggins is very dull, I assure you.'

Unfortunately his words were immediately contradicted by Nanny Piggins doing a run of tumbling acrobatics from one side of the garden to the other, so athletically impressive and perfectly performed she would have won a gold medal for gymnastics if she could ever bother turning up to the Olympics.

'Where did she learn to do that?' asked the journalist.

'At the circus, I suppose,' muttered Mr Green. 'She used to work there.'

'Let me get this right,' said the journalist. 'You're running for public office even though you hired a circus pig to be your nanny, and she's running against you?'

'What's wrong with that?' asked Mr Green.

'And you don't know what's wrong with that,' added the journalist, writing this all down. 'This story gets better and better. I've got to interview her.'

'No you don't,' protested Mr Green. 'I won't allow it.'

'What's that over there?' asked the journalist, pointing to the doorway.

Mr Green turned to look, but when he looked back, the journalist had wrenched open the window and dived headfirst out into the azalea bushes. (This was normally something Nanny Piggins only did when Mr Green launched into one of his many long and boring monologues on the power of compound interest.)

'Nanny Piggins, I wondered if I might ask you a few questions,' called the journalist as she hurried across the yard.

'I'm not saying anything until my lawyer gets here,' declared Nanny Piggins. (Isabella Dunkhurst had trained Nanny Piggins to reflexively say this after her last disastrous brush with the law.)

'I'm not a police officer, I'm a journalist,' said the journalist.

'Then I'm not saying anything until a very large cake gets here,' said Nanny Piggins. 'I'm a big believer in chequebook journalism. If you ring Hans' Bakery and use my name, he will give you a ten per cent discount.'

'It's the least he can do,' added Michael. 'Nanny Piggins paid for his holiday to Barbados last year.'

'His lemon tarts were particularly delicious last year,' explained Nanny Piggins. 'He earned every penny and deserved a relaxing break after making all that lemon custard.'

'Mr Green tells me you're his nanny,' said the journalist.

'That's progress,' said Nanny Piggins. 'Usually he denies it.'

'And these are his children?' asked the journalist. 'I didn't realise he had children.'

'Yes, he usually denies that too,' agreed Nanny Piggins.

'Are they adopted?' asked the journalist.

'What adoption agency would give a man like that three children?' scoffed Nanny Piggins.

'It's easier to believe than a woman ever marrying him,' countered the journalist. 'No offence,' she added to the children.

'None taken,' said Derrick. 'We often wonder the same thing ourselves.'

'I'm standing right here, I can hear you!' complained Mr Green.

'Well, go inside and fetch us all some chocolate milk,' suggested Nanny Piggins. 'That way you won't have to listen to all the things we are going to say about you.'

'But you will say nice things, won't you?' pleaded Mr Green.

'Mr Green,' chided Nanny Piggins. 'It is wrong to lie. Especially in front of children. It's not my fault that you're a terrible father. It's your fault. If this journalist asks me about it, I shall just have to tell the truth.'

Mr Green clutched his head in his hands. 'I knew I should never have agreed to this interview at home.'

Fortunately for Mr Green, at that moment the journalist noticed something even more bizarre than a circus pig working as a nanny or the fact that Mr Green had managed to get some poor woman to marry him. She noticed that the ground was vibrating, rhythmically, in a long drawn-out rumble, every three seconds.

'Why is the ground shaking?' asked the journalist.

'It isn't,' said Nanny Piggins. She had been living with Mr Green so long, she had slipped into thinking all humans could be so easily fooled.

'You just said you couldn't lie,' said the journalist.

'No, I didn't,' said Nanny Piggins.

'Yes, you did,' said the journalist.

Nanny Piggins abandoned reasoned (or, in this case, unreasoned) argument at this point and simply stamped on the journalist's foot.

'Ow!' yelped the journalist.

'Children, fetch me something pointy,' said Nanny Piggins. 'I might need to drive this woman off.'

'Nanny Piggins, you're on your last warning with the Police Sergeant,' reminded Samantha. 'It's bad enough that you are always going around kidnapping or being kidnapped by your circus colleagues, but if you assault a journalist, he's going to be so cross.'

'But if we bang her on the head she might get amnesia,' argued Nanny Piggins.

'She might get brain damage,' countered Derrick.

'No-one would ever notice in a journalist,' pouted Nanny Piggins.

'Why is that shed right up against the back of the house?' asked the journalist.

'None of your business,' said Nanny Piggins.

'I bet that violates planning regulations,' said the journalist.

'Oh no,' whimpered Mr Green. He might be unscrupulous about hiring untrained circus pigs to look after his children, but he hated the very thought of being caught breaking a rule.

'I'm going to have a look,' said the journalist.

But she did not get to. Instead, she got a better

feel for the vibrations in the ground, because Nanny Piggins knocked her over in a flying crash tackle.

'I'm not letting you,' declared Nanny Piggins.

'Wow, you could play for the Dulsford Mules,' said Michael, seriously impressed.

'I'm calling the police!' exclaimed the journalist, pulling a mobile phone out of her pocket.

'No, you're not,' said Nanny Piggins, grabbing the phone and, with pinpoint accuracy, lobbing it into Mrs Simpson's compost heap.

The journalist was just about to pull Nanny Piggins' hair and Nanny Piggins was just about to bite her shin (something that often happens to journalists, because they are such shocking busybodies), when they were interrupted by the deafening WHOOP-WHOOP-WHOOP sound of a helicopter swooping down above them.

'Crikey,' said the journalist. 'I'm either about to be swept off to a secret location, never to see my family again, or this story is so good it's going to be above the fold on the front page.'

Two people dressed all in black and carrying backpacks full of equipment abseiled down from the helicopter and landed in the Green's backyard. The helicopter swooped away.

'Cool!' said Derrick.

'Is everyone all right?' asked a black-clad woman as the man with her took out a computer and various pieces of monitoring equipment and started setting them up.

'This unprincipled charlatan has given me a nasty grass stain on my frock,' accused Nanny Piggins, 'but apart from that I think we're all okay.'

'We're from the NSMI,' said the woman.

'The National Scrummy Macaroon Inquiry?' asked Nanny Piggins, 'because I'm not giving up my recipe, no matter how much they beg.'

'No, we're from the National Seismic Monitoring Institute,' explained the woman. 'We've registered a constant flux of earthquakes from this location. Has anybody been hurt? Is there any structural damage to your home?'

'No, it's reinforced with Mars Bars,' said Derrick.

'This is the epicentre of the earthquakes,' said the male researcher, looking up from his equipment, 'but the cause doesn't seem to be seismic.'

'How can that be?' asked the woman. 'The vibrations are so strong.'

'It appears to be coming from that shed,' said the man.

'I suppose if I bonked everybody on the head,

I wouldn't be lucky enough for them all to get amnesia,' sighed Nanny Piggins.

There was nothing she or the children could do to stop the journalist, Mr Green and the researchers as they walked towards the shed, then peered in through the window. There was a moment's pause as their brains processed what they were seeing. Then the journalist was the first to speak, or rather scream, 'Aaaaaaggghhh! There's a giant bear!'

Then pandemonium broke out. Mr Green ran for the house with an amazing turn of speed. It quite impressed Nanny Piggins. But then he totally nullified the good impression by locking the back door – locking his own children outside, undefended against a giant bear (we know Boris was a loving warm-hearted bear, but Mr Green did not).

The NSMI researchers leapt over the fence into Mrs McGill's garden, where they were both knocked unconscious by Mrs McGill's home defence system. She threw baked bean tins at their heads. (Mrs McGill had played in the women's professional baseball league during the war, so she had a very good fast ball.)

The journalist scrambled over the other fence into Mrs Simpson's yard and took off down the street.

'Oh dear,' said Samantha, slumping to the floor so she wouldn't have far to fall when she inevitably fainted from hyperventilating.

'What are we going to do?' asked Michael.

'Right,' said Nanny Piggins. 'We've got about five minutes before the journalist raises the alarm and the authorities get here.'

'Animal Control?' asked Derrick.

'The Police Sergeant?' asked Michael.

'Either that or someone from the local insane asylum,' guessed Nanny Piggins. 'We've got five minutes to wake Boris up and get him out of there.'

'How are we going to do that?' asked Derrick.

'Derrick, you shinny up the drainpipe, climb in through the upstairs bathroom window and get the oscillating fan from my bedroom,' instructed Nanny Piggins.

'I'm on it,' said Derrick as he sped away. (He'd become quite good at shinnying drainpipes since Nanny Piggins had become his nanny.)

'Michael, go into the laundry and use a crowbar to pull up the floorboards,' said Nanny Piggins.

'Why?' asked Michael.

'Because the laundry is the one room of the house my brother never goes into, because he doesn't wear clothes,' said Nanny Piggins, 'so that is where

I hid his birthday present – a 200-litre drum of the finest honey.'

Two minutes later Nanny Piggins had set up the fan and Michael had rolled out the drum of honey.

'How is this going to wake up Boris?' asked Samantha.

'Open the shed window,' instructed Nanny Piggins as she levered open the lid of the drum. As soon as the smell wafted up, the children immediately understood Nanny Piggins' plan.

'You're going to smell him out!' exclaimed Derrick.

'Exactly,' said Nanny Piggins. 'Turn on the fan.'

Michael turned on the fan and the delicious waft of honey floated across the yard and in through the shed window.

'How long will this take to work?' asked Michael.

'Oh, I should think –' began Nanny Piggins, but she didn't have to finish her sentence because at that moment the shed exploded into a thousand pieces as Boris leapt to his feet and launched himself at the drum, shouting, 'Honey!'

Eighteen seconds later, having drunk all the honey, it looked like Boris might now go into a sugar-induced coma, but Nanny Piggins was not standing for that.

'Boris,' she declared, shaking him by the paw, 'you have to get out of here before the authorities come for you.'

'I just want a nap,' protested Boris sleepily.

'He's never going to budge,' said Derrick.

'I know how to motivate my brother,' said Nanny Piggins. 'Boris, I heard that the retired Army Colonel who lives round the corner is having honey sandwiches for afternoon tea.'

The children barely saw Boris leave. He was a blur of movement, too fast for their eyes to register as he leapt over the fence and took off.

When Animal Control, the Police Sergeant and the media turned up, there was nothing for them to see except a nanny and three children reconstructing a shed (reinforced with Mars Bars).

Nanny Piggins accused the journalist of concocting the whole story to sell papers; the seismic researchers assumed that the whole thing had been a hallucination as the result of an inner ear disturbance caused by too much abseiling; and Mr Green just did what he always did – pretended the whole thing never happened.

When Boris returned home late that night, the now reinforced shed was back in its regular spot. Boris was feeling very cheerful, having eaten half his body weight in honey (and that was a lot of body weight), so naturally he settled down for a lovely nap.

'What if he starts snoring again?' asked Michael.

'I've been thinking about that,' said Nanny Piggins as she watched her brother snooze. 'I've come up with a new, simplified plan. Obviously we'll still bake 3240 cakes. But next time, instead of soundproofing the whole shed, we'll just break off a little bit of one cake and soundproof our ears.'

# CHAPTER 5

## Nanny Piggins and the Happy News

Nanny Piggins and the children were sitting around the dining table eating breakfast. Mr Green was also there, but they knew from experience that if they focused purely on the delight of chocolate-covered Belgian waffles served with chocolate sauce and chocolate ice-cream on the side, they could forget about him entirely.

Normally Mr Green was happy with this arrangement. He liked forgetting about the existence of his children too. In fact, he was able to do it for several days, or even weeks at a time, and without even the aid of chocolate-covered waffles. But on this particular morning Mr Green did not want to be forgotten. He was smirking and chortling in the way that some people do when they have something they want to rub another person's nose in. He was on his fifth 'haw, haw-haw' when Nanny Piggins put down her spoon and turned on him.

'Spit it out then!' she demanded.

Mr Green flinched.

'And when I say spit it out,' continued Nanny Piggins, 'I don't mean spit out that horrible high-fibre muesli you insist on eating. I mean spit out whatever it is that you so obviously desperately want to say. I have spent many, many years perfecting my chocolate-covered waffle recipe. King Albert the second of Belgium himself awarded me that country's highest honour, the Knighthood of the Order of Leopold, for my creation. So I will not have the waffle-eating experience of these children soiled by your pathetic attempts to strike up a conversation.'

It shows how much Mr Green desperately wanted to say what he had to say because he resisted the opportunity to denounce Nanny Piggins for being rude. (He could confidently assume that she would give him opportunity to do that again later.) So he did spit it out. 'Have you seen the news this morning?' he smirked.

Nanny Piggins and the children groaned. Mr Green was so awful at making conversation it was terribly painful when he tried to protract the experience by being cryptic. 'Obviously I have neither seen, nor heard, nor read the news,' said Nanny Piggins. 'I made Belgian waffles for breakfast.' Nanny Piggins indicated the huge platter of waffles in front of her and the children. 'As if I would go to all the trouble of making something so supremely delightful, then ruin the whole experience by finding out what was going on in the rest of the world today. Unless the entire rest of the world made themselves Belgian waffles too, I don't want to know about it.'

'The morning news bulletin will be on in five minutes,' continued Mr Green. He was undeterred because he had stopped listening to Nanny Piggins and was just waiting for her to stop speaking so that he could start again (something many men do). 'You should watch. I think you will find it very interesting.' At this point Mr Green actually giggled. I would say he giggled like a schoolgirl but that would not be true. If you hear a school-girl giggle it is a perfectly pleasant sound (in moderation). But hearing Mr Green giggle was so revolting it actually made Nanny Piggins feel slightly sick, and therefore put her off finishing her chocolate-covered waffles. Naturally she fought this instinct and ate the waffles anyway, but the joy of the whole experience had definitely been ruined.

Nanny Piggins sighed. 'I suppose we might as well watch the news now,' she said. 'Waffles do not taste as good when your father is talking, and he is obviously intent on gloating about something so we had better find out what it is so we can take appropriate retribution.'

At this point Mr Green stopped smirking. He had been in such a rush to irritate Nanny Piggins he had entirely forgotten to put on his shin pads, and he had learnt from bitter experience that it could be very painful to irritate Nanny Piggins without wearing this essential protective equipment. 'I've got to go to the office,' said Mr Green, with which he leapt up and sprinted from the room.

'Your father is a very strange man,' said Nanny Piggins.

'So are we going to watch the news?' asked Michael.

'We'd better,' said Nanny Piggins. 'I don't want

him to ruin another meal. I'm planning chocolate mousse for dinner.'

They trooped into the living room, still licking chocolate off their hands, fully expecting to see that their father had done something silly like hold a press conference announcing his intention to close the local children's hospital, or rip up all the trees along the main street, or push old ladies onto the road, or something equally morally bankrupt. But sadly it was nothing that pleasant. For a start they had to sit through five utterly miserable and bleak stories about a famine in North Korea, a war in the Middle East, a famine and a war in Africa, and a celebrity who almost died after drinking too much bottled water.

'I don't think there's anything on the news relevant to us at all,' denounced Nanny Piggins. 'I think your father has just tricked us into watching the news as a cruel joke to make us depressed and afraid of water.'

At that moment a more familiar face flicked onto the screen. It was Mr Green. He had evidently held a press conference earlier that morning.

'I am bringing these important documents to light, about the true character of my mayoral opponent Sarah Matahari Lorelai Piggins,' announced Mr Green.

'Is it the secret to how she makes her hair so bouncy and gorgeous?' called a female reporter from the front row.

'Is it her chocolate cake recipe?' called a heavy-set older journalist from the back.

'Is it photographs of her sunbathing in a bikini?' called a young journalist who had been hopelessly in love with Nanny Piggins ever since she had slammed into him one time while running home with arm loads of butter to make croissants.

'No, no, no. I have documents proving that Sarah Piggins is a convicted criminal,' began Mr Green.

In the Green house, Nanny Piggins leapt up and started yelling at the television. 'But I was given a full pardon because the judge was insane!'

Sadly at the press conference, recorded earlier, Mr Green could not hear Nanny Piggins so he continued. 'She regularly associates with known jailbird Mr T. Ringmaster . . .'

'Only when he kidnaps me,' argued Nanny Piggins.

'. . . and she broke into a maximum security prison!' concluded Mr Green.

'But only because I was hungry for Chinese food,' wailed Nanny Piggins.

Mr Green looked very smug and proud of himself on the television screen.

'Is that all?' asked a senior journalist.

'What do you mean "Is that all?",' cried Mr Green. 'She's a serial criminal! A menace to society!'

'Her cakes are tasty though,' called out a younger journalist.

The other journalists murmured their agreement.

Nanny Piggins switched off the television. 'I've had enough of that,' she declared.

'Would you like us to fetch your hot-pink wrestling leotard so you can go and punish Father?' asked Michael.

'No, I'm not upset with your father,' said Nanny Piggins.

'You're not?' asked Samantha. 'He was very rude.'

'He defamed you publicly,' said Derrick.

'But is it defamation when it's all true?' asked Michael.

'Yes,' said Derrick.

'Then he definitely defamed you,' Michael agreed.

'Of course he did,' said Nanny Piggins. 'I would expect nothing less from such a small man. And when I say "small" I obviously do not refer to his waistline, because that is quite large. No, Mr Green is small of spirit, brain and common sense. He is not worthy of me spending half my day chasing him about town in my hot-pink wrestling leotard just because he is too silly to stand still and let me bite his shins.'

'Really?' asked Samantha, surprised at her nanny's uncharacteristic magnanimity.

'No, I'm angry with the news for broadcasting such a pile of bleak misery,' declared Nanny Piggins.

'You mean the truth,' asked Derrick.

'Precisely,' said Nanny Piggins. 'I'm going to go down there and put a stop to it.'

'But you were going to drive us to school today,' Samantha reminded her.

'Obviously you can't go to school now,' said Nanny Piggins. 'We have an outrage to rectify.'

Michael did not say anything, he just beamed with pleasure. They were going to dissect broccoli in his class today, so he was very happy to miss that.

'You will have to come with me,' said Nanny Piggins. 'If I am going to tell these news people off I shall need your support. You can bring a thesaurus to help me think up extra rude things to yell at them.'

A few minutes later Nanny Piggins, Boris and the children pulled up outside the local television station. It was a very unimpressive establishment. A windowless, concrete single-story building with the words *Dulsford Community Television Station* hand-painted on the outside.

'Are you sure this is the television station?' asked Nanny Piggins, consulting the map.

'The sign says it's a television station,' said Derrick.

'But it's so unimpressive,' said Nanny Piggins. 'Perhaps it's a ruse, and really it's the headquarters for an international branch of wicked super-spies.'

'I think even naughty international super-spies, who would do anything to avoid being arrested by Interpol, would still have too much pride to work in such a rundown building,' said Boris. Being a Russian ballet dancer, he knew lots of international super-spies because they were always going under-cover as ballet dancers.

Nanny Piggins kicked in the front door of the TV station. She actually had to, because the steel door had rusted and swollen shut.

'Right, I'm taking over this institution,' she announced as she strode into the studio. Nanny Piggins was impressive at the best of times but none more so than when she was wearing her hot-pink wrestling leotard.

'Ssshhhh, we're in the middle of a bulletin,' hissed the floor manager.

'All the more reason for me to intervene,' said Nanny Piggins. 'I saw your last bulletin and it was an abomination to the good name of television. How dare you sully the same airwaves that bring us joyful programs like *The Young and the Irritable* and *The Bold and the Spiteful*.'

'Those shows always make you cry,' pointed out Derrick.

'Yes, but I enjoy doing it,' said Nanny Piggins. 'These news bulletins just make everybody unhappy. And think of the poor people who watch the news while they eat dinner – it would totally ruin their food. And I cannot abide anybody who ruins food.'

'Excuse me,' said the newsreader, giving up any attempt to keep reading the news. 'I've been reading the news here for eight years, and I just want to say – this pig is entirely right!'

'Hear, hear,' agreed Nanny Piggins.

'The news is always miserable,' continued the newsreader. 'Some nights I have to pinch myself in the leg to stop myself from bursting into tears in the middle of the broadcast.'

Boris burst into tears. He could tell he had met a kindred spirit.

'If she's got some way to cheer up the bulletin, please let her do it,' said the newsreader. 'It's so hard to get out of bed in the morning when I know I've got to come into work and read all this sadness.'

Boris immediately rushed over and gave the newsreader a big hug. 'You poor man,' said Boris. 'The thought of going to work in the morning makes me want to cry too. That's why I live in a garden shed and only teach a few afternoon ballet classes to earn my pocket money.'

'We can't let a pig burst in here and take over,' protested the news director, emerging from the control booth. 'We have a civic responsibility to report the news.'

'To who?' asked Nanny Piggins. 'The few poor souls who have broken the channel-changing knob on their televisions? No-one is watching this drivel and the people who are watching aren't paying attention.'

'You can't change the editorial policy of the station without consulting the board of directors,' argued the news director.

'I'll make a bet with you,' said Nanny Piggins. 'I bet if I change the editorial policy the board won't notice because they don't watch this station either.'

'But you're running for mayor,' continued the news director. 'People will be cross if we let you take over.'

'Why?' asked Nanny Piggins. 'They should be impressed by initiative and leadership.'

'But what about the rest of the bulletin?' asked the floor manager. 'This is going to air and we haven't finished yet.'

'Let me finish it,' said Nanny Piggins.

The newsreader happily got out of her way so he could go and weep with Boris in the corner.

'Just read what is on the autocue,' the floor manager told her.

Nanny Piggins settled herself in the chair, picked up the sheets of copy on the desk, then tossed them away over her shoulder and ignored the autocue entirely. 'Good evening, I am mayoral candidate Sarah Matahari Lorelai Piggins,' began Nanny Piggins, 'and I am taking over this news bulletin because I think the journalists here are a bunch of old misery guts who should be ashamed of themselves. So this is the news according to me. Earlier today, the Queen of England went to the Battersea dog shelter and adopted a thousand puppies. Then she threw Prince Andrew out of his palace and let the dogs live there.'

'I like puppies,' murmured the newsreader between sobs.

'In South America,' continued Nanny Piggins, 'the President of Brazil sent a bag of Brazil nuts to every citizen in his country as a thank-you present for electing him in the first place'.

'What a nice man,' said Boris, dabbing his eyes.

'And in Papua New Guinea a remote group of tribeswomen discovered the cure for the common cold,' said Nanny Piggins, 'but decided not to tell anyone because they think it is fun to stay in bed eating chocolate and watching daytime television when you have a runny nose. And now for the weather.'

Nanny Piggins turned and looked at the weather man.

'Tomorrow in Dulsford the weather will be cold and wet,' said the weather man.

'No, it won't!' interrupted Nanny Piggins. 'It will be warm and sunny all day, until four o'clock in the afternoon when there will be a very brief shower, so we can all put on our rainboots and jump in puddles.'

'But according to the synoptic charts . . .' protested the weather man.

'The viewers do not want to know about your sinuses, thank you,' said Nanny Piggins, 'so from everyone here at the Dulsford News Team, especially me, mayoral candidate Sarah Matahari Lorelai Piggins, goodnight.'

'Clear,' called the floor manager.

'Not a word you said is true,' protested the news director. 'Not the news bulletin, not the weather, you even said goodnight when it is 10 o'clock in the morning!'

'Pish,' said Nanny Piggins. 'Other types of television are all made up, like soap operas and medical dramas, so why not make up the news?'

'What is she talking about?' asked Boris. 'What does she mean, saying soap operas are made up?'

'Don't worry yourself about it,' said Samantha. 'Just put your paws over your ears for a few minutes.'

'You can't fictionalise the news,' argued the news director.

'Why not?' asked Nanny Piggins.

'Because . . . because . . . it's the news!' wailed the news director.

'Come now,' said Nanny Piggins. 'I've heard more reasoned arguments from three-year-olds.'

'It's jolly good of the Queen to adopt all those puppies,' said the newsreader.

'But she didn't,' yelled the news director. 'This pig just made it up.'

The newsreader looked like he was about to cry. Nanny Piggins wrapped him in a big hug.

'There you go,' said Nanny Piggins to the news director. 'This is exactly what you do to your viewers every day. You wear them down and make them upset. Life is hard enough. When people get home and turn on the television, they do so to find relief. The last thing they want is truth and reality. We get more than enough reality from reality, thank you very much.'

'This is crazy,' said the news director.

'Of course it is,' said Nanny Piggins. 'Crazy people have all the best ideas. Look at Leonardo da Vinci, total genius, designed a helicopter in the sixteenth century. But it was four hundred years before the invention of the aviation fuel to power it. Talk about nutty as a fruitcake! Hold on a minute – why are we standing around arguing? Derrick, be a dear and run out to the car and fetch a cake. No, better make that a dozen large cakes, of the chocolate variety.'

Nanny Piggins rightly judged that once they had eaten a slice of her cake, the news director and his television crew would capitulate and give her anything she wanted. After the first mouthful they were begging her to give up her mayoral aspirations and become a television executive instead.

When eleven o'clock rolled around the crew were still eating, so they let Nanny Piggins read the news again. This time she did not make up any news stories at all. She just dictated her recipe for chocolate cake and recounted the time the crown prince of Spain tried to elope with her because he had fallen desperately in love with her apple strudel.

'This can't go on,' said the news director, licking chocolate icing from his fingers before helping himself to another slice. 'You can't just read out recipes. You have to do some news.'

'But that cake recipe *was* news,' argued Nanny Piggins. 'Using chocolate-flavoured butter, chocolate milk and six bars of molten chocolate was a breakthrough in the development of bakery.'

'At the 12 o'clock bulletin we must report some actual news,' argued the news director.

'Don't worry, I've got it covered,' said Nanny Piggins. 'I've already called a few friends to drop in and help us out.'

At ten minutes to twelve the entire cast of *The Young and the Irritable* turned up.

'Darlings!' cried Nanny Piggins with delight. 'It's so good to see you.' (Nanny Piggins had once been the head writer of *The Young and the Irritable*. For more information, see Chapter 8 of *Nanny Piggins and the Daring Rescue*.)

'Where's the cake?' asked the actor who played Vincent. 'You told us there would be cake if we arrived before noon.'

'And there will be,' promised Nanny Piggins. 'I just need you to do a little bit of acting for me first.'

What followed was spectacular, because now Nanny Piggins was reading the news and crossing to live dramatisations acted out by her soap-opera-star friends.

The actor who played Vincent played the head of the Water Quality Authority, who was responsible for a thousand tonnes of ping pong balls falling into the ocean. He gave a passionate speech accepting all the blame, but explaining that he made the terrible mistake because he was in love with the woman who checked his gas meter.

Then the woman who checked his gas meter burst into the studio (she was being played by the actress who played Bethany) and declared that she wasn't really a menial water board employee, she was actually the head of police on a sting operation to entrap him. But she had found no evidence because he was blameless, and instead had fallen deeply in love with him.

The news bulletin ended with a ten-minute session of them kissing passionately, in between looking off into the middle distance and talking about how lucky they were to have found each other.

For the one o'clock bulletin, Nanny Piggins got Buff Senior and Buff Junior to play political rivals who gave up on reasoned debate and settled their differences by stripping off their shirts and combatting in professional wrestling.

And in the two o'clock bulletin, the actress who played Sabrina pretended to be the prime minister of Turkey, and sang a heartbreaking ballad about how devastated she was to learn that the prime minister of Turkey did not get to eat roast turkey every day for lunch.

Between all the cake and the heady atmosphere of drama and requited love, even the crew started to really enjoy themselves. Broadcasting the news had never been so much fun. It was such a relief to have a day with no talk of car accidents, war or politics. Everything was going swimmingly until the real boss, the chairman of the board of directors, burst into the studio.

'What on earth is going on here?!' demanded the chairman of the board.

'Um . . .' said the news director. On hearing the question put so plainly, he suddenly realised it would sound foolish to say they had let a pig take over the news and make everything up.

Fortunately Nanny Piggins came to his aid. 'Do not blame your staff. If they showed any weakness of character it is purely because of their low blood sugar levels because you, as their employer, failed to provide adequate doughnuts in the break room. Therefore, I have hijacked this newsroom in the name of happiness, to prevent them from broadcasting any more misery-inducing stories about reality or what mean people are doing to each other in far distant countries.'

'Well, whatever you're doing,' yelled the chairman, 'keep it up! The ratings have gone through the roof. They've doubled with each bulletin. There were 67 people watching the 9 o'clock bulletin.'

'That would be my mum and her friends at the nursing home,' said the floor manager. 'They like to watch so they can laugh at me when I come to visit.'

'Now there are tens of thousands of people tuning in,' continued the chairman. 'With ratings like that we'll actually be able to attract advertisers and give everyone pay rises.'

'These workers don't want pay rises,' protested Nanny Piggins.

'Yes we do,' protested the workers.

'Okay, yes they do,' conceded Nanny Piggins. 'But more importantly they want doughnuts, and chocolate biscuits and real coffee, or better yet hot chocolate in the break room.'

'And perhaps a window?' suggested the floor manager. 'I ended up in hospital last year from vitamin D deficiency.'

And so the *Dulsford Community Television Station* became the first television news service to entirely fictionalise the news (although tabloid newspapers had been doing a similar thing for years) and specialise solely in happy news, with the guarantee of at least one declaration of love and wedding per bulletin. It was a huge success. News stations around the world syndicated their program or copied it outright. And in show business, there is no higher form of flattery than plagiarism and violating someone's copyright.

'Will you stay and oversee the transformation of our news service?' asked the chairman.

'I'd love to,' said Nanny Piggins, 'but I'm afraid I have an even more vitally important job, looking after these three children.'

'Plus you're running for mayor,' Michael reminded her.

'Oh yes, that too,' agreed Nanny Piggins. 'I think of that more as a silly hobby than an actual job.'

'You'd better not mention that in any of your campaign speeches,' suggested Derrick.

# CHAPTER 6

## *Nanny Piggins and the Vacant Lot*

Derrick was sitting quietly in his science class trying to pretend he knew what kinetic energy was when Nanny Piggins burst into the room (demonstrating kinetic, potential and sound energy in one dramatic move). She scanned the room and spotted him.

'Derrick, you must come with me immediately. It is a matter of the utmost desperate urgency,' exclaimed Nanny Piggins as she strode over and started to help Derrick gather up his things. (She then threw them out the window because where they were going he would not be needing school books.)

'Hang about, what's going on?' asked the teacher. 'You can't just pull Derrick out of class without written permission.'

'But there has been a dreadful tragedy,' sobbed Nanny Piggins.

'Father?' asked Derrick.

'No, no,' said Nanny Piggins, struggling to hold back tears. 'Something far worse.'

The teacher was a man, and a scientist, so he was doubly uncomfortable with displays of emotion. The last thing he wanted was for a lady pig and a young boy to burst into tears in his classroom. His cat had died the previous week and if he saw other people crying it would set him off too. And if his class saw him cry he just knew they would never hand their homework assignments in on time again. So he ushered Derrick and Nanny Piggins out of the classroom as fast as he could, promising to send a memorial wreath as soon as possible.

Nanny Piggins did not stop with Derrick. Next they went to Samantha's classroom and dragged her away from the clutches of a well-meaning student teacher. Then Michael was fetched simply by pulling him out a window when his teacher's back was turned.

'What's going on, Nanny Piggins?' asked Derrick. 'What's happened that is so bad?'

'Is there a warrant out for your arrest?' asked Samantha.

'Is the Ringmaster trying to kidnap you?' asked Michael.

'Did you accidentally break into the Slimbridge Cake Factory and eat all their finger buns again?' asked Derrick.

'Oh no,' said Nanny Piggins. 'This is a real tragedy – something that affects us all. It will devastate the community if we don't do something right now.'

'Tell us all about it from the beginning,' suggested Derrick.

'I was at the library this morning,' began Nanny Piggins.

'But what about the restraining order?' interrupted Michael.

'That says I mustn't go *in* the library. It doesn't say I can't stand outside the door and yell things,' said Nanny Piggins. 'And just this morning I thought of some really good rude names to yell at the head librarian so I had to go down to try them out.'

'Did they work?' asked Michael.

'I don't know,' admitted Nanny Piggins. 'The

head librarian wouldn't come out of her office. But the junior librarian jotted them all down and promised to send them to the head librarian in a memo.'

'And how did that lead to tragedy?' asked Samantha.

'While I was yelling through the front door of the library, I happened to notice their window display, where the council posts all the plans for their new development projects.'

'Like when they're building new shopping centres and stuff?' asked Michael.

'If only they were building something as benevolent as a shopping centre,' lamented Nanny Piggins. 'I'm afraid our local council is doing something a thousand times more wicked.'

The children struggled to imagine what Nanny Piggins could think was so wicked.

'Not a . . .' Samantha hesitated to use the next word because she knew it had a strong effect on her nanny, 'a bacon factory?' she asked.

Nanny Piggins flinched in horror. 'Good lardy cakes, nothing that bad. What an atrocious thought. No, but definitely something terrible.'

'What is it?' asked Derrick.

'You know the vacant lot on Hazelnut Street?' asked Nanny Piggins.

'Yes,' said the children.

'Well the council is going to turn it . . .' said Nanny Piggins, pausing for emphasis, 'into a park!'

'A car park?' asked Michael.

'No, a park,' said Nanny Piggins.

'You mean a public park?' asked Derrick.

'With swings and play equipment?' asked Samantha.

'Yes, exactly,' said Nanny Piggins.

The children all looked at each other. They were not sure how to assimilate this information. Derrick spoke first. 'But Nanny Piggins, surely a new park is a good thing?'

'But what about our vacant lot?' said Nanny Piggins. 'I looked at those plans closely. They are not making any promises to build another one somewhere else. If they go ahead with this "park" plan there will be no vacant lots in easy walking distance of our house.'

'The vacant lot on Hazelnut Street is covered in builders' rubbish and weeds,' said Michael.

'And burnt-out cars,' said Samantha.

'And there's an open stormwater drain running through the middle,' said Derrick. 'At night-time the whole place is crawling with rats.'

'I know,' said Nanny Piggins, 'which is what makes it such a wonderful place to explore with children. There is so much scope for imagination and role play. On a swing you just swing. But in a burnt-out car you can pretend to be a runaway pig escaping from the law.'

'Why do you need to pretend?' muttered Michael. 'That's what you do most days.'

'In the stormwater drain you can pretend to be convicts chained together and on the run from bloodhounds,' said Nanny Piggins.

'But there is a danger of flash flooding,' said Derrick.

'And big weedy bushes and builders' waste are perfect for pretending to be soldiers attacking the enemy's cake factory to cut off their supply,' said Nanny Piggins.

'But if there is a park, there will be flowers and lawn,' said Samantha. 'It will look very nice.'

'Hah, nice,' scoffed Nanny Piggins. 'Anywhere can be nice. But being a thrilling playground for the imagination is not so easily achieved.'

'So why did you pull us out of school?' asked Michael. 'Not that I'm complaining. I wasn't really enjoying learning about the exploration of river tributaries.'

'So we can put a stop to it, of course,' said Nanny Piggins.

'How?' asked Samantha, desperately hoping her nanny's answer would not be something that involved chaining herself, or others, to a bulldozer.

'According to council regulations, a development plan can be stopped immediately,' said Nanny Piggins. 'All you need is ten thousand signatures on a petition.'

'Ten thousand!' exclaimed Derrick.

'I know, it's not many, is it?' said Nanny Piggins. 'Just five thousand each if we get Boris, split into two groups and get started right now, I'm sure we'll have a couple of thousand by dinnertime.'

Sadly Nanny Piggins' epic optimism was somewhat deflated when they met again around the kitchen table just seven short hours later.

'How many signatures did you get?' asked Michael as his nanny slumped down in her chair and started comfort eating the raw cake ingredients she found in the cupboard.

'None,' said Nanny Piggins sullenly.

'Not even the people she threatened to bite,' said Samantha.

'Not even the people I did bite,' added Nanny Piggins.

'Well, we did better than that,' said Boris proudly.

'You did?' asked Nanny Piggins, immediately perking up.

'Yes,' said Boris. 'We got one signature.'

'Really?' said Samantha. Seven hours of door-knocking had made her realise that the general population was in fact very pro-parks and anti-rat infested vacant lots. 'Who was the one signature?'

'Mrs McGill next door,' said Derrick.

'She hit Boris over the head with her handbag first,' said Michael.

'She didn't hurt me physically,' said Boris with a sniff, 'but she did hurt my feelings.'

'But then when she found out we wanted her to sign a petition about the park she cheered up,' said Derrick. 'She signed it right away.'

'She says the sound of children enjoying them-selves gives her a migraine,' explained Michael.

'But she wouldn't be able to hear children in a park six blocks away,' said Samantha.

'Yes, but she says she would know they were there enjoying themselves and to her mind that would be just as bad,' explained Michael.

'I don't like to abandon anything,' said Nanny Piggins, 'particularly babies. I know it worked for Moses' mother when she put him in a basket and set him afloat on the Nile but, as a general rule, leaving infants with no discernible nautical skills in charge of a vessel is a bad idea. That instance aside, in this case, I think we are going to have to abandon the petition.'

'Does that mean we have to go to school tomorrow?' asked Michael.

'Of course not,' said Nanny Piggins. 'Tomorrow you must help me prepare.'

'You're not going to go and buy a long chain, are you?' asked Samantha, envisioning the bulldozer scenario becoming ever more likely.

'No,' said Nanny Piggins. 'I need to prepare some really good arguments. There is going to be a public meeting next week when members of the general public can tell the council what we think of their wicked plans to vandalise our beloved play area.'

'You've started coming up with arguments already, haven't you?' guessed Michael.

'Yes,' said Nanny Piggins. 'Fortunately I have a long list of colourful insults because I can re-use the ones I prepared for the head librarian. It would be a shame to let such evocative imagery go to waste.'

It was a full three days until the meeting, so Nanny Piggins had a lot of time to read the speeches of Winston Churchill regarding his determination to win World War II, and listen to the speeches of various professional wrestlers regarding who they were going to tear apart with their bare hands. So when she arrived at the meeting, she was fully prepared to eviscerate her local council members with her cutting wit or leap on them in an atomic pile driver, whichever felt more appropriate in the moment.

What Nanny Piggins did not realise was that the councillors knew a thing or two about not listening to their local constituents. These public meetings were held every month and the councillor in charge of the subcommittee on public consultation (the least important councillor in council) would always give a long and boring talk about fiduciary responsibility, or water rates, or something equally boring so that anyone planning to complain would be put to sleep or be totally exhausted with the dreariness of it all and therefore keep their own comments short.

Finally, after a two-and-a-half-hour report on the installation of a drip system in the sewage treatment plant's garden, the councillor threw the meeting open to the floor when he asked for 'any other business'.

Surprisingly, Nanny Piggins did not immediately leap to her trotters. It took the children a couple of seconds to wake her up by waving a coffee cake in front of her snout. So the first person to the microphone was Nanny Piggins' arch nemesis, Nanny Anne.

'I'd like to complain about the plan to build a park on the Hazelnut Street vacant lot,' said Nanny Anne.

Nanny Piggins rubbed her ears. 'Am I dreaming,' she asked, 'or has the polarity of the entire planet reversed? Because I can't think of any other earthly reason why Nanny Anne would be championing my argument.'

'Shh, just listen,' said Derrick.

'What's the basis for your objection?' asked the councillor.

'I don't want there to be a park because parks are too dirty,' said Nanny Anne.

'Phew,' said Nanny Piggins. 'For a moment there I thought she was going to say something reasonable.'

'But there are going to be beautiful flowerbeds and lawns,' said the councillor.

'The lawns are the worst bit,' protested Nanny Anne. 'If there are lawns, children will sit on them or, even worse, run across them and fall over. Have you ever tried to get a grass stain out of a pair of white espadrilles?'

'I can't say that I have,' conceded the councillor.

'And flowers will only lead to bees and where there are bees there is honey,' continued Nanny Anne.

'Mmm honey,' said Boris.

'. . . and honey is packed full of sugar, which causes childhood obesity,' said Nanny Anne, 'and I don't see how you can stand by and encourage childhood obesity.'

'But the children will run around the park and burn off energy,' said the councillor.

'Not if they've been raised properly, they won't,' said Nanny Anne. 'Running is undignified. Thieves run. And people who are late.'

Nanny Piggins leapt to her trotters. 'Nanny Anne is a raving lunatic,' she declared.

'Hear, hear,' agreed the councillor.

'But in this instance I agree with her,' said Nanny Piggins. 'These plans to build a park are morally bankrupt. But for the opposite reasons Nanny Anne has given. A park is wrong because there is no way a park can be as fun as a vacant lot.'

'Within the last three months, four children have been taken to hospital with head injuries, one with a tetanus infection and two with rat bites and all from the Hazelnut Street vacant lot,' said the councillor, reading from his notes.

'Which just goes to show how much they must love playing there,' said Nanny Piggins. 'I remember my first tetanus infection. In hindsight it was silly to tap-dance on a bed of nails, but at the time it was a lot of fun.'

'The park is going ahead,' said the councillor. 'We've been given a grant by the Ethel Baumgarten Society for the Beautification of Suburban Areas. We can't spend the money on anything else so it will be spent on this.'

'Please, for the sake of the children, can't you embezzle the funds and run off to Brazil,' pleaded Nanny Piggins, 'or has your job in local government entirely robbed you of any initiative?'

'It is going ahead,' declared the councillor firmly, 'and we have been given a generous grant. Apparently the children in this area have the seventh highest rate of asthma, and the fifth highest rate of vitamin D deficiency in the country, and therefore particularly inspire the pity of wealthy benefactors. So we are doing this properly. We have hired a leading expert in the international study of children's play to be a consultant on the project.'

'You've hired an adult who has spent his whole life watching children?' asked Nanny Piggins. 'Why couldn't you just flush the cash down the toilet like a normal lunatic?'

'Dr Higgenbottom is a leader in his field,' said the councillor.

'Hah! So he's a world leader in waffle,' scoffed Nanny Piggins. 'If I had a PhD in shim-sham I wouldn't be boasting about it. When does he get here?'

'He flies in from Geneva tomorrow,' said the councillor.

'What was he doing in Switzerland?' asked Nanny Piggins. 'Advising them to move the alps three inches to the left to improve their feng shui?'

'Actually he was advising them on –' began the councillor.

'It was a rhetorical question,' said Nanny Piggins. 'You're not meant to answer rhetorical questions. You're just meant to accept that you've been insulted. Now, when is this snake-oil salesman going to inspect the site?'

'I can't give you the details of our private meeting,' said the councillor.

'What about the Freedom of Information Act?' demanded Nanny Piggins.

'People have a right not to be harangued by pigs,' countered the councillor.

'Not when they are going to ruin my favourite vacant lot, they don't,' declared Nanny Piggins.

'I'm not telling you when the meeting is,' yelled the councillor.

'I'll find out,' said Nanny Piggins. 'I don't like being unpleasant. But I'm very good at it and if that's what it takes, I'll do it.' Nanny Piggins started to strip off her dress to reveal her wrestling leotard underneath (which had the words *Nanny 'The Crusher' Piggins* emblazoned in diamantes across her chest).

'You really would be better off if you just told her,' said Derrick kindly.

'You're being a nuisance,' accused the councillor. 'I've got a good mind to call the police and have you removed from this meeting.'

'Go ahead,' challenged Nanny Piggins, 'but I'm one step ahead of you. I never go to a public meeting, auction or library without a two-kilogram box of shortbread biscuits in my handbag, especially for bribing the police.'

'Nanny Piggins, remember you promised the Police Sergeant you would stop telling people you bribe him,' reminded Samantha.

'I meant "coax" the police to see my point of view,' amended Nanny Piggins.

'This meeting is adjourned,' called the councillor, banging a gavel on the fold-up table.

'You can't do that!' said Nanny Piggins.

'Yes, I can,' said the councillor. 'It is in the rules for public meetings. As soon as a member of the public physically threatens me I can call the meeting to a close. So thanks to you I can get home in time to eat my reheated dinner while watching *The Young and the Irritable* with my wife.

'I will admit,' said Nanny Piggins as they walked home, 'that I feel slightly guilty about berating the councillor. If he likes *The Young and the Irritable*, he is clearly a man of discerning taste.'

'So you are going to abandon your opposition and let the council go ahead and build their beautiful park?' asked Derrick.

'Goodness, no!' exclaimed Nanny Piggins. 'It

would be wrong to allow them to proceed with such senseless vandalism. I think I shall have to persuade this international expert to see my point of view.'

'How are you going to do that?' asked Michael.

'A good hard bite on the shins ought to do it,' guessed Nanny Piggins.

'But you don't know when he's going to inspect the park,' said Samantha.

'We'll just have to camp there until he turns up,' said Nanny Piggins.

'But our tent blew away when you tried to convert it into a hot-air balloon by strapping the kettle barbecue underneath and filling it with hot air,' Derrick reminded her.

'A double tragedy,' said Nanny Piggins sadly. 'We lost the tent and we haven't had toasted marshmallows since but never mind, at the vacant lot we can sleep in one of the burnt-out cars.'

'But what about the rats?' protested Samantha.

'I'll bake them a cake,' said Nanny Piggins. 'They won't want to bite us after they've tried my raspberry ripple delight cake.'

'Will we get some too?' asked Michael. He liked anything with the words ripple or cake in it.

'Of course,' said Nanny Piggins. 'I can't have you biting the rats out of jealousy.'

So Nanny Piggins, Boris and the children spent the night camping in a burnt-out car on the vacant lot. To be strictly accurate they spent about 45 minutes camping on the vacant lot. By the time they had baked all the supplies Nanny Piggins felt were necessary for a night of camping, then baked another batch of supplies because they had so thoroughly 'tasted' the first batch, then packed it all up in Nanny Piggins' travelling trunk, along with several gripping novels and complete changes of clothes for any eventuality – Nanny Piggins felt it was vitally important that a person should be prepared for a white-tie ball at a moment's notice – they eventually stepped out their front door at 5.45 am.

It then took them an hour and a half to walk the six blocks to the park, partly because the travelling trunk was so heavy to drag, but mainly because they got so engrossed in a very enthusiastic game of hide-and-seek along the way. Nanny Piggins managed to squeeze through Mr Mahmood's cat-flap and hide in his kitchen. And because none of the children thought to look in a locked house, and Nanny Piggins was thoroughly engrossed in eating the entire contents of Mr Mahmood's fridge, it took some time for them to find her. It was only when Mr Mahmood came downstairs to breakfast and discovered that Nanny Piggins had drunk all the milk that they heard his telltale yelling and guessed where she was.

Fortunately he was soon placated by a half share of a raspberry ripple delight cake and they arrived safely at the vacant lot at 7.45. They had only just rolled out their sleeping bags and set up their camp fire when three white cars drew up alongside the vacant lot.

'Who could that be?' wondered Derrick.

'Perhaps they've come to burn out their cars,' guessed Nanny Piggins. 'That would be good. There are already three burnt-out cars here. If there were another two, we could have one each to sleep in.'

'It's the councillor,' exclaimed Samantha as grey-suited men began to emerge from the vehicles.

'What are you doing here?' demanded Nanny Piggins rudely.

'What are *you* doing here?' demanded the councillor.

'This is public land. I have every right to be here,' stated Nanny Piggins boldly.

'No, actually it's not,' said the councillor. 'It won't become public land until it becomes a park. So technically you're trespassing.'

'I'm not tres-passing,' said Nanny Piggins, 'I'm tres-staying because I'm not passing anywhere until this issue is resolved.'

The councillor sighed. 'Please just go home. Dr Higgenbottom is going to be here any minute and I don't want you to embarrass me in front of him.'

'Don't worry,' said Boris. 'Nanny Piggins never sets out to embarrass anyone else. She would only ever embarrass herself.'

'And I don't embarrass easily,' said Nanny Piggins. 'After spending years of being blasted out of a cannon and having people look up my dress, it takes a lot to mortify me.'

Just then another car pulled up.

'Out of interest,' said Nanny Piggins, 'were you planning to burn out these cars? Because if you did I think they would make a fine addition to this vacant lot.'

The councillor rolled his eyes. 'We are building a park, not adding to the waste on a vacant lot.'

'All right,' said Nanny Piggins, 'but I know which would be quicker. Five gallons of petrol and a lit match and my improvements would be done with.'

They watched as the car door opened and a tall, heavy-set man wearing a strange-coloured suit got out.

'Is that suit red?' asked Derrick.

'It looks almost pink,' said the councillor.

'I think you'll find the technical name for that colour is "blush",' said Nanny Piggins, 'or, as the laymen say, "dark pink".'

'What sort of man wears a pink suit?' wondered the councillor, beginning to suspect that perhaps he had made a horrible decision.

'What sort of man has the word "bottom" in his name and doesn't get it changed by deed poll?' asked Nanny Piggins.

'Would you like me to ask him?' asked Boris. 'He's coming this way.'

'Dr Higgenbottom,' said the councillor, holding out his hand, 'I'm Councillor –'

'Aaa-aaa-ah,' said Dr Higgenbottom. 'Stop right there. I am a creative. I can't have my head filled with meaningless details.'

'I was just going to tell you my name,' said the councillor.

Dr Higgenbottom held up his hand for silence again. 'Enough. I'm here to create a vision, a space that will improve the lives of the children in this town for decades to come. I can't have my head filled with empty words.'

'I told you so,' said Nanny Piggins smugly. 'I've never met anyone with a PhD whose head wasn't largely empty.'

'I knew I should have worn my earplugs,' sighed Dr Higgenbottom, turning to the scurrying assistant behind him. 'Sebastian, is there some way we could get these people to stop talking.'

'Shhh,' said Sebastian sharply, with his finger across his lips, in case the rudeness of his shushing was not immediately apparent.

'Samantha,' whispered Nanny Piggins. 'Remind me to bite both of them before they get back in their car.'

'I'm ahead of you,' whispered Samantha, for she already had out her notepad and was jotting a reminder note for her nanny which said just that.

Nanny Piggins, Boris, the children and the councillor stood and watched as Dr Higgenbottom and Sebastian strode about the park. Dr Higgen-bottom stared at things, lay down on the concrete, jumped up and down in the water of the stormwater drain, licked a burnt-out car and generally behaved like a nitwit while Sebastian took photographs and measurements.

'Do you think he really is a doctor,' asked the councillor. 'He seems to be behaving like a lunatic.'

'There is no doubt in my mind that he is both,' said Nanny Piggins wisely. 'He is clearly a lunatic because what he is doing is barking mad. But he is clearly a PhD because anyone with a lesser qualification who carried on like this would have been locked up years ago.'

After fifteen minutes of eccentric behaviour the doctor and his assistant returned.

'My report is ready,' said Dr Higgenbottom.

'Don't you need time to go away and write it up with photos, graphs and spreadsheets?' asked the councillor.

'I don't work in government – that's your job,' said Dr Higgenbottom. 'I have reached my verdict. Of all the thousands of public spaces I have been asked to inspect, in dozens of different countries around the world, I have never before seen one like this. It is absolutely and utterly . . . perfect. There is no need to change a thing. Except perhaps you could add a couple more burnt-out cars.'

'I knew it!' exclaimed Nanny Piggins. 'The man is a genius.'

'But it is dangerous, unsafe and rat-infested,' protested the councillor.

'As is life,' said Dr Higgenbottom. 'This park has wonderful scope for the imagination. There is opportunity for water play, interaction with small mammals and role-play games using found objects.'

'You mean there's a drain, rats and rubbish,' summarised the councillor.

'Exactly! This park has everything,' gushed Dr Higgenbottom. 'For the sake of the children, I forbid you to change a thing. Sebastian, give the man his invoice, we're leaving.'

Sebastian slapped a sheet of paper into the councillor's hand and they left. The councillor slumped down on the bonnet of a burnt-out car.

'What am I going to do?' he asked. 'I've been given a two-million dollar budget to improve this park and I've got nothing to spend it on.'

Nanny Piggins felt sorry for the councillor. 'Don't worry. Why don't you just hire another advisor? One who will be more cooperative.'

'But where am I going to find another person with a PhD in children's playgrounds,' asked the councillor.

'I doubt you'll find a second person quite that silly,' agreed Nanny Piggins. 'Why don't you hire me? I am the world's leading flying pig. Amazing and delighting children comes as naturally to me as breathing in and out.'

'She's telling the truth,' confirmed Michael. 'She amazes and delights us every day.'

'Sometimes she horrifies and shocks us as well,' added Samantha, 'but she always makes us the most delicious cake afterwards to help us get over it.'

'Plus Nanny Piggins only charges ten cents an hour,' added Derrick.

'And it's only going to take me one minute to tell you how to spend your budget,' said Nanny Piggins.

'It will?' asked the councillor, beginning to feel a glimmer of optimism.

'Obviously you can't change a thing that is here,' said Nanny Piggins, 'but you could add to it.'

'Add to it?' asked the councillor, liking the idea. 'How?'

'Really, the only way I can think of improving this already wonderful public play area is by building a state-of-the-art ice-cream shop slap bang in the middle,' stated Nanny Piggins, stamping her trotter on the very spot she thought suitable.

Everyone gasped, the way people instinctively do gasp when they know they have just heard a brilliant idea.

'Ice-cream and playgrounds go together like . . .'

said Nanny Piggins, 'well, like cake and more cake.'

So that is exactly what the councillor did. And because Nanny Piggins was a generous soul, she even agreed to allow some of the budget to be spent on planting flowerbeds, because everyone liked looking at flowers and lawn, and because she knew how much it would upset Nanny Anne.

The Hazelnut Street Park soon became the most popular park in Dulsford, because even the most scrupulous parent can overlook a few rats and a stormwater drain when they had a double scoop of chocolate ice-cream with extra sprinkles in their hand.

# CHAPTER 7

## *Nanny Piggins and the Last Cake of the Romanovs*

Nanny Piggins, Boris and the children were very bored. There was no reason why they should have been – they were standing in the Russian embassy, and usually embassies are fascinating places. You never know what sort of spies, important dignitaries or looted art is hidden away inside. And even if none of those things is there, Nanny Piggins enjoyed pretending they were. Her imagination was so vivid that playing a game where you pretend to cause an international incident was almost as much fun as actually causing an international incident. If anything it was more fun, because it tended to result in less jail time.

But on this occasion they were not enjoying themselves, because they had not come to the embassy to apologise for destroying a national treasure or beg for the release of a much loved circus colleague. They had come for a much more tedious reason – to renew Boris' passport.

There is something about the bureaucracy of passport dispensing, that even in this day and age of computers, digital photographs and holographic watermarks, it still takes weeks for a government to issue a small cardboard book with a photo stuck inside. And even though they could easily have the television on in the waiting area (perhaps playing re-runs of *The Young and the Irritable*) or hire a juggler to amuse the waiting applicants (goodness knows you would not have to pay them very much; unemployment among professional jugglers is sadly very high, over a hundred and ten per cent), passport officials seem to take pride in ensuring the boredom of all those who enter their office. And passport applicants are always so anxious that they may have committed some terrible transgression, like signing their name outside the box, getting their birthday wrong or smiling in the photograph, that they are overcome with boredom due to the stress of the situation.

It is a strange fact that you are only ever bored if you are stressed. If you are relaxed and content, you can happily lie on a beach doing nothing for hours. But five minutes in a line at the passport office feels like five hours of being hit about the head by a wet fish.

Normally Nanny Piggins would have alleviated the boredom by handing around some cake to everyone in the office or loudly denouncing the inefficiency and inhumanity of the staff; but on this occasion Boris had made her promise that she would behave, because he really did want a passport.

'I don't understand why you want a passport anyway,' grumbled Nanny Piggins. 'You don't need one. Whenever you travel internationally it's almost always because you've been kidnapped. And if you are stuffed inside a crate with a pillowcase over your head, the customs officials aren't going to check your paperwork.'

'I want a passport,' said Boris, 'because I want one. I like to think that one of these days I shall rise to a sufficient level of dignity and respect in the community that someone will pay for me to sit in an airline seat like a regular law-abiding person.'

'You could always pay for a ticket yourself,' Michael pointed out.

'Don't be ridiculous!' exclaimed Boris. 'If I had that kind of money, of course I'd spend it all on honey. I am a bear, after all.'

'I didn't know bears could get passports,' said Samantha.

'We can in Russia,' said Boris. 'Bears are held in very high regard. We have a long historic association with Russian folklore. Plus, we tend to bite people who are rude to us.'

'Следующий,' called the grey grumpy woman behind the counter (which is Russian for 'next').

'It's me, it's me, it's my turn,' said Boris excitedly as he skipped up to the counter. 'I'm applying for a passport.'

'Urgh,' said the grumpy woman (which means 'urgh' in Russian) as she started paging through the voluminous application form and tutting ominously at any misspellings or places where Boris had accidentally smeared honey on the document.

'Would you just get on with it,' snapped Nanny Piggins. 'We have been waiting here for ages and if my blood sugar drops any lower I may have to resort to eating one of the stale sandwiches you have in your vending machine.'

The children gasped. In the entire time they had known Nanny Piggins, they had never known her to eat anything as low in sugar as a sandwich. So they knew she was desperately serious.

'You. Bear. Stand on line,' ordered the grumpy woman. There was a line of masking tape stuck on the carpet, where applicants had to stand to get their passport photo taken.

'I think you forgot to say please,' Boris reminded her kindly.

'You want passport. You stand on line,' snapped the grumpy woman.

Boris raised his eyebrows. 'I think Mr Manners needs to pay a visit to this embassy.' But he went and stood on the line.

'You too tall,' accused the woman as she looked through the camera at Boris' chest.

'How can you be too tall to get a passport? That's heightism!' accused Nanny Piggins. She knew she should be behaving herself but there was something about this official. She was so rude that Nanny Piggins had an overwhelming urge to bite her shins.

'Get down on your knees,' the grumpy woman ordered Boris.

'I don't suppose you have a little cushion I could kneel on?' asked Boris politely.

'No cushion for you!' declared the grumpy woman.

At this point Boris, predictably, started to cry.

'How dare you upset my brother!' accused Nanny Piggins.

'I adjust lights,' said the grumpy woman, whipping out three spotlights and quickly adjusting them so they glared into Boris' face, making him wince.

'Perfect!' she declared and took the photo.

'That's a hideous photograph!' accused Nanny Piggins as she peered across the counter to see the grumpy woman's computer screen.

'Now you go away!' ordered the grumpy woman.

'Come on, Sarah,' sniffed Boris. 'I want to go home. My feelings have been hurt.'

But as they turned to leave, the Russian embassy's Head of Security was blocking their exit.

'It is you!' accused the Russian Head of Security as he pointed at Nanny Piggins.

'Yes, yes, it is me,' said Nanny Piggins. 'The World's Greatest Flying Pig. I can sign an autograph for you later. But right now would you kindly step aside. Listening to all this Russian is making me hungry for Briskvit.' She turned and explained helpfully to the children, 'That's a moist Russian sponge cake.'

'That's not what he means. Look!' said Derrick as he pointed to a noticeboard on the wall. There were signs warning travellers about the dangers of smuggling caviar (the tins can explode in your suitcase and make your underwear very smelly), the health risks of travelling to Siberia (mosquito bites in summer and hypothermia in winter), and ten sheets of paper, each showing a picture of one of Russia's ten most-wanted criminals. The seventh picture was unmistakeably of Nanny Piggins.

'They've found me!' yelled Nanny Piggins. 'Quick, run!'

Unfortunately embassies are not designed for making speedy exits. There are security guards and checkpoints everywhere. And while they are mainly focused on keeping lunatics with bombs *out*, it is a simple matter for them to turn around and keep lunatic pigs *in*.

'We're surrounded,' panicked Samantha.

'Quick, Boris!' cried Nanny Piggins. 'Distract them.'

'How?!' asked Boris.

'I don't know,' said Nanny Piggins. 'Do some ballet!'

'They're Russians,' protested Boris. 'They see world-class ballet all the time.'

'Yes, but not performed by a ten-foot-tall Kodiak bear,' argued Nanny Piggins.

'Are you saying people only watch my ballet because I'm a bear?' said Boris, starting to get teary.

'Of course not,' said Nanny Piggins, back-pedalling frantically. 'I just meant that it is even more impressive that you are a world-class artist given that you are so tall.'

But it was too late. Boris was weeping so hard and so loudly, he could not hear anything else. Fortunately, however, a ten-foot-tall bear collapsing in a heap on the floor and bawling his eyes out is even more distracting than a sublime ballet perfor-mance, so Nanny Piggins and the children were able to dodge around the befuddled guards and make good their escape.

A short time later, Nanny Piggins and the children were at home, under the kitchen table and eating cake while Nanny Piggins tried to come up with a plan.

'Why are we under the table?' asked Samantha, taking a bite of delicious Victoria sponge.

'In case any Russian agents look in the window to try to see us, of course,' said Nanny Piggins.

'But why did we come home?' asked Derrick. 'Surely this is the first place they will look.'

'But they don't know our address,' argued Nanny Piggins. 'And I made very sure that we weren't followed. That is why we took such a circuitous route home, through every bakery in the district.'

'I thought you were just hungry for cake,' said Michael.

'Of course I was,' said Nanny Piggins. 'Running away always builds up my appetite.'

'There is one slight problem,' said Boris through a mouthful of honey cake. (He had escaped and walked straight home while the guards were busy being told off by the Russian Head of Security for letting a wanted criminal get away.)

'What?' asked Nanny Piggins. 'Have you eaten all the honey cake again?'

'No,' said Boris. 'The cubic metre of cake you made me is the perfect-sized snack for a growing bear. No, the snag is, they will probably be able to figure out our address.'

'How?' asked Nanny Piggins.

'From the passport application I left lying on the counter,' said Boris.

'You left that behind?!' exclaimed Nanny Piggins.

'I really want a passport,' protested Boris.

'Oh dear, oh dear, oh dear,' said Nanny Piggins, her mind racing. 'I'm just going to have to initiate emergency evacuation plan D.'

'What's that?' asked Derrick.

'I'll have to run away and join the French Foreign Legion,' said Nanny Piggins.

'Do they still have that?' asked Michael.

'And do they take women?' asked Samantha.

'And do they take pigs?' asked Derrick.

'What right-minded military institution would turn me away?' asked Nanny Piggins. 'A pig with my artillery experience is invaluable. And I quite fancy moving to Algeria. They make very good sweet biscuits there called *Halwat Eeba*, which are filled with dates.'

'But what about us?' asked Michael.

'I'm sure the Foreign Legion will take you,' said Nanny Piggins, giving him a hug. 'Legionnaires lie about their real names and ages even more than actresses.'

'I won't do it!' declared Samantha.

'What?!' said everyone else. It was unlike Samantha to be so bold.

'I won't do it!' declared Samantha again. 'I don't want to join the military, I don't want to learn to speak French, I don't want to lie about my age and I don't want to move to Algeria.'

'You say that now,' said Nanny Piggins, 'but only because you've never tried *Halwat Eeba*. It's very good.'

'There must be some other way you can avoid deportation to Russia,' said Samantha.

'Perhaps if you explained to us exactly what you did to get in trouble in the first place,' suggested Derrick.

'You know how much I hate going to museums,' began Nanny Piggins. 'Well, it was a rainy day in St Petersburg and I was wearing the most darling suede slingback shoes. Obviously I couldn't keep walking about outside and risk stepping in a puddle.'

'It would be a crime against footwear,' agreed Boris.

'I had no choice,' said Nanny Piggins. 'I had to take shelter indoors, but the nearest building was the Hermitage Museum.'

'You poor thing!' exclaimed Boris.

'What's the Hermitage Museum?' asked Michael.

'It is the largest and most impressive art gallery in the world,' explained Boris. 'It is full of all the great Russian masterpieces as well as important works by Leonardo da Vinci, Raphael, Michelangelo, Caravaggio and all the other super famous artists.'

'In short,' said Nanny Piggins, 'it is a dreadfully tedious place. And I was stuck inside being forced to wander past one miserable painting after another until it stopped raining outside.'

'So what did you do to get in trouble?' asked Derrick. 'Did you bump into something?'

'Or accidentally smash something?' asked Samantha.

'Or purposefully smash something?' asked Michael.

'No,' said Nanny Piggins, with a note of shame in her voice. 'I ate something.'

'What?' asked Derrick suspiciously.

'One of the exhibits,' confessed Nanny Piggins.

'You ate a priceless artwork?!' exclaimed Derrick.

'I'm afraid so,' admitted Nanny Piggins. 'It was not my proudest moment.'

'What did you eat?' asked Samantha. 'Not a Leonardo da Vinci painting? There's no way we could come up with a money-making scheme to replace that.'

'No,' said Nanny Piggins. 'I ate a Greta Pleveski.'

'A who what?' asked Derrick.

'Greta Pleveski was the greatest Russian artist of the early twentieth century,' continued Nanny Piggins. 'I was wandering through a particularly gaudy gallery of baroque portraiture when I smelled her masterpiece.'

'You smelled it?' queried Samantha.

'My trotters were drawn to the enticing aroma,' continued Nanny Piggins. 'I walked down the corridor into a small and dimly lit gallery featuring one artwork, displayed on a central plinth, beneath a lone spotlight.'

'What was it?' asked Michael. 'A sculpture?'

'A painting?'

'An antique?'

'It was the last cake of the Romanovs!' declared Nanny Piggins.

The children sat silently for a moment as their brains processed this . . . until they realised that none of them had any idea what their nanny was talking about.

'You're going to have to explain,' said Derrick.

'The Romanovs were the last emperors of

Russia,' said Boris. 'They enjoyed untold wealth and the most lavish luxury ever seen, and all while the Russian people suffered poverty, hunger and even slavery.'

'So what happened?' asked Michael.

'Well, the people got sick of the poverty, hunger and slavery,' explained Nanny Piggins. 'They rose up and overthrew the Romanovs.'

'Where does the cake come in?' asked Derrick.

'On the day they were overthrown, the Romanov family were just sitting down to have morning tea – and the Romanovs did not do things by half measures. They had the finest cake maker in the world, Greta Pleveski, make them a chocolate cake. And not just an ordinary chocolate cake either. A fifteen-tier chocolate cake with exquisite handmade sugar decorations depicting an exact replica of the Winter Palace in winter. It was the most beautiful cake ever made.'

'Then why didn't the Romanovs eat it?' asked Michael.

'The Bolsheviks started bombing the palace and they had to flee by train before they could even take the first bite,' explained Nanny Piggins.

Boris burst into tears.

'Why are you crying?' asked Samantha.

'I know the Romanovs were dreadfully mean to

all the poor people,' said Boris, 'but it just seems so cruel not to let them eat their cake.'

'When the Bolsheviks raided the palace the cake was still sitting on the coffee table,' said Nanny Piggins. 'It was put in the Hermitage Museum as a monument to the selfish extravagance of the aristocracy.'

'So why on earth did you eat it?' asked Derrick.

'Because it smelled so good!' wailed Nanny Piggins. 'You know how good my sense of smell is! How could I be in the same room and resist such a wonderful chocolate cake?'

'But the Russian Revolution took place in 1917,' said Derrick. 'The cake must have been 90 years old!'

'It was still delicious!' declared Nanny Piggins. 'The icing was so thick it created a vacuum inside, so it was very well preserved.'

'But Nanny Piggins,' said Samantha, 'what you did was terrible. You destroyed a great work of art and a historically significant artefact.'

'Pish!' said Nanny Piggins. 'The greater crime was letting the cake go uneaten! Cake is not like a painting you hang on a wall to get dusty and faded. A cake is to be tasted, chewed, swallowed and enjoyed. That is its purpose. The greatest purpose of all. To deny such a fine cake to yield to its higher destiny is a crime. It's a desecration of a great artist's master-piece. If Greta Pleveski were alive today she would have begged me to eat it. She would have picked up a cake fork and eaten it herself.'

'So you just reached over and took a bite?' asked Michael, in even greater awe of his nanny's audacity than he had ever been.

'Not quite,' admitted Nanny Piggins. 'I had to jump over a red velvet rope, smash through two-inch thick bulletproof glass and disable a state-of-the-art alarm system by bashing it with my shoe.'

'So the slingbacks got ruined anyway?' asked Boris.

'I'm afraid so,' said Nanny Piggins.

'What happened next?' asked Samantha.

'I've been running from the KGBCD ever since,' said Nanny Piggins.

'What's the KGBCD?' asked Derrick.

'Well you know what the KGB is?' asked Nanny Piggins.

'The Russian secret police?' asked Derrick.

'Yes,' said Nanny Piggins, 'and the KGBCD is their cake division.'

'I thought the KGB was disbanded after the collapse of the Soviet government,' said Derrick.

'They kept up their cake division,' said Nanny Piggins. 'They take their desserts seriously in Russia.

They reserve the most ruthless tactics for dealing with cake-related crime.'

Suddenly there was a loud pounding at the door.

'Piggins, we know you're in there!' the Russian Head of Security boomed from outside. 'We have the house surrounded. Come out now, before we are forced to do structural damage to your home.'

'Agh, please don't let them take you, Sarah. What will I do without you?!' wailed Boris. 'Who will explain the bits I miss in *The Young and the Irritable* when I cry too loudly to hear what's going on?'

'No-one is taking me anywhere,' declared Nanny Piggins, 'because I had the foresight to install an ejection system!'

'You did?' asked the children.

'Yes, one night when I snuck down to the kitchen for a little midnight cake, I had the brilliant idea of using the fireman's pole in reverse, as the trajectory controller for a massive rocket launcher.'

'Really?' said the children.

'It was a simple matter really,' said Nanny Piggins. 'All I had to do was install a remote-controlled trap door in the roof, get a custom-made harness, and a massive rocket powerful enough to blast me up into the sky.'

As she spoke, Nanny Piggins opened the secret compartment in the laundry floor (the one where she stored honey). She brought out the rocket backpack and harness, which she went over and clipped to the fireman's pole.

'We're coming in!' yelled the Russian Head of Security as he kicked in the door.

'Goodbye!' declared Nanny Piggins. 'I'll write to you when I get to Algeria.'

With that, she fired up the rockets on her backpack and, in an explosive burst, shot up through the house.

The Russian agents, the children and Boris peered up through the ceiling and out through the trapdoor in the roof where they could see Nanny Piggins hurtling ever upwards into the far blue sky.

'She escaped!' said Samantha.

'We are going to be in so much trouble when the Kremlin finds out about this,' said the Russian Head of Security.

'Hmm,' said Boris. 'I'm not so sure.'

'What do you mean?' asked Derrick. 'Look at her. She's miles away.'

'Yes,' agreed Boris, 'but she has gone miles directly upwards. My sister has very few failings but one of them is not thinking two moves ahead.

True, she has brilliantly escaped the house and these cunning Russian agents.'

'You think we're cunning?' said the Russian Head of Security. 'That's very kind. I don't suppose you could write an endorsement for our website?'

'But I suspect that she has not put as much thought into what she would do next,' continued Boris.

'What do you mean?' asked Michael.

'Nanny Piggins has blasted several miles directly upwards,' explained Boris, 'but gravity working as it does, surely she is going to come straight back down.'

They all peered back up through the hole in the roof again. Nanny Piggins was a tiny dot way up in the sky. But slowly the dot started to get larger, and larger.

'Boris is right!' exclaimed Michael. 'She's coming straight back down.'

'Quick,' called the Russian Head of Security. 'Fetch a net!'

'Quick!' called Boris, 'Fetch some sponge cake!'

'Why?' asked Samantha. 'If she falls ten miles out of the sky she's not going to be hungry.'

'I bet she will be,' said Michael.

'The cake is not to eat,' said Boris. 'She needs something soft to land on.'

The children ran outside with armfuls of cake.

The agents rushed out with a giant net. But Nanny Piggins was one step ahead of them all. Realising her strategic error and dangerous predicament, Nanny Piggins had used the prevailing winds to push her towards a safe landing. (Her years of experience in plummeting made her very good at this.) So as they all rushed out into the street hoping to stop Nanny Piggins from hitting the bitumen, she saved herself by neatly landing in Mrs Lau's fish pond with a huge KERSPLASH!

'She isn't dead!' yelled the children with delight.

'Pah-pah-pah!' said Nanny Piggins as she spat out pond water. 'My hair does smell of fish poo, which is almost as bad.'

At that moment the Russian agents threw a huge net over Nanny Piggins.

'Piggins, you are under arrest,' announced the Russian Head of Security. 'We will be extraditing you to Russia to face trial for your crimes against national security.'

'Very well,' said Nanny Piggins resignedly, holding out her wrists to be handcuffed. 'Hang on a minute. What did you say I'd done?'

'You published top-secret photographs that compromised national security,' said the Russian Head of Security.

Nanny Piggins rubbed her snout. 'I don't remember ever doing that. Admittedly I have suffered amnesia on more than one occasion due to my tendency to get unpleasant head injuries, but usually when I snap out of the stupor I find I have just spent the time eating cake or perhaps chocolate. I don't usually become a photographer and expose state secrets. What state secret did I expose exactly?'

The Russian Head of Security looked sheepish. 'You published a photograph of the president in his underwear.'

'I did?' said Nanny Piggins.

'And you didn't warn him you were about to take a photograph so he didn't have time to suck in his tummy first,' said the Russian Head of Security.

'That can't have been my sister,' said Boris. 'She would never be that cruel.'

'So this has nothing to do with Nanny Piggins eating the last cake of the Romanovs?' asked Michael.

'What?' asked the Russian Head of Security.

Nanny Piggins quickly put her trotter over Michael's mouth to silence him. 'Don't mind him,' said Nanny Piggins. 'He doesn't know what he's saying. His blood sugar is low.'

Samantha suddenly had a brainwave. 'Are you sure you've got the right Piggins?' she asked.

'Of course,' said the Russian Head of Security. 'We have her picture right here.'

The Russian Head of Security produced a mugshot of a very guilty-looking Nanny Piggins.

'Maybe you aren't looking for Nanny Piggins,' said Samantha. 'Maybe you are looking for one of her identical fourteenuplet sisters. You do realise that this is Sarah Matahari Lorelai Piggins.' Samantha pointed to her nanny.

'You're not Beatrice Piggins?' asked the agent.

'No, I am not!' said Nanny Piggins. 'That's my morally bankrupt sister.'

'Is Beatrice worse than Wendy the evil super-spy or Katerina the lover of vegetables?' asked Michael.

'She is more fun than Katerina but she is more amoral than both of them put together, for Beatrice is a member of the paparazzi,' declared Nanny Piggins. 'She specialises in taking embarrassing pictures of politicians and publishing them in the newspaper.'

'So that's not you?' asked the Russian Head of Security.

'No,' said Nanny Piggins.

'Oh dear, we're going to be in trouble,' said the Russian Head of Security. 'I don't suppose you have an address for your sister then?'

'My sisters and I don't keep each other's postal

addresses. We aren't big on sending Christmas cards,' said Nanny Piggins, 'but I think I can work out where she might be.'

'Where?' asked the Russian agent.

'You have to understand that my sister Beatrice has a genius for hiding,' said Nanny Piggins.

'All her sisters are geniuses at one thing or another,' supplied Michael.

'In her job as a paparazzo Beatrice has perfected the art of hiding in bushes, sneaking behind parked cars and gluing rubbish all over her clothes so that she can creep up on unsuspecting celebrities,' explained Nanny Piggins. 'She could be here right now and you'd never know it.'

They all looked about at the bushes, parked cars and postboxes to see if any of them could be a disguised pig.

'But she's not,' continued Nanny Piggins. 'You have to think the way she would think. The best place to hide is the very last place a team of Russian agents would ever think to look for her.'

The Russian agents looked at each other. 'You'll have to give us a clue,' said the Russian Head of Security.

'The Russian embassy!' declared Nanny Piggins.

'Really?' asked the children.

Twenty minutes later they were all standing in the lobby of the Russian embassy, again.

'Where is she?' asked the Russian Head of Security.

'Right there!' declared Nanny Piggins as she spun around, leapt over the counter and wrestled the grumpy passport clerk to the ground. And let me tell you it was quite a wrestling match. It was immediately apparent that Nanny Piggins was entirely right and that the Russian official was in fact one of her identical fourteenuplet sisters. And not just because as soon as Nanny Piggins knocked her wig and glasses off they looked exactly alike, but because they were so evenly matched at wrestling. They rolled about on the floor, putting each other in leg locks and beating each other about the head with staplers and other office equipment for a full twenty minutes, before Nanny Piggins called a truce so that they could have a cake break.

'But how did you know it was me?' asked Beatrice.

'It was the passport photo that gave you away,' said Nanny Piggins. 'It was so awful. No mere government official could make someone look that bad in a passport photo, only a photographer of extraordinary ability could pull it off.'

'Thank you,' said Beatrice. 'So few people appreciate the artistry involved in making someone look dreadful.'

'But why would you risk coming here?' asked Derrick. 'It's a lot of trouble to go to, to take a bad passport photo.'

'The passport photo was just for fun,' said Beatrice. 'I am on a mission.'

'A mission?!' exclaimed Nanny Piggins. 'Don't tell me you're a top-secret super-spy too. It's bad enough that Wendy is.'

'No,' said Beatrice. 'I'm on a photography mission. A bounty has been put on your head.'

'Really?' asked Nanny Piggins, looking up to see if there was a Bounty chocolate bar sitting on her head that she had not noticed previously.

'Not that type of bounty,' said Derrick.

'Good,' said Nanny Piggins. 'I would be ashamed to be walking around with a chocolate bar on my head and not having eaten it.'

'Word has gone out in the paparazzi community that one of your political rivals . . .'

'Let me guess,' said Nanny Piggins. 'Mr Green?'

'I don't know,' said Beatrice. 'He used a fake name to protect his identity – Mr Greenway.'

'That sounds like your father's level of imagination,' said Nanny Piggins.

'Anyway, he let it be known that he would pay top dollar for a compromising photograph of you,' explained Beatrice.

'You would sell-out your own sister?!' said Nanny Piggins. 'I'm appalled. How much for?'

'Fifty dollars' worth of chocolate,' said Beatrice.

'Oh, well that's entirely understandable then,' said Nanny Piggins. 'I'll tell you what. I'll pose for a compromising picture if you split it with me.'

'All right,' said Beatrice happily.

And so Nanny Piggins and her sister set up the most compromising situation they could imagine. Beatrice took a photo of Nanny Piggins eating a salad sandwich.

'Won't it ruin your image?' asked Samantha.

'It's unparalleled hypocrisy,' agreed Boris.

'It could damage your campaign,' warned Derrick.

'Pish! It won't hurt my image one jot,' said Nanny Piggins. 'Anybody who knows me will know that it could not possibly be true and it must have been digitally altered.'

# CHAPTER 8

*Nanny Piggins and the Great Debate*

'You are both blithering idiots. I'm astounded that you have not been locked in high-security institutions for the criminally stupid,' yelled Nanny Piggins.

She was preparing for the mayoral debate – a televised event that took place before each election. Normally candidates would present their own policies and point out inadequacies in the policies of their opponents. But Nanny Piggins had a much more spectacular debating style.

'There's no such thing as institutions for the criminally stupid,' argued Derrick. He was pretending to be the incumbent, Mayor Bloomsbridge, which was very brave of him because he did get hit in the head by slices of cake whenever Nanny Piggins became too cross to express what she was feeling with words alone.

'Well then, there should be, if for no other reason than to keep the likes of you two off the streets,' yelled Nanny Piggins. (The shopkeeper who did not like parking meters had dropped out of the race. Or, rather, she had been dropped off at prison after she was caught using an angle grinder to cut down every parking meter on the main street in the middle of the night.)

'How do you intend to confront the rising crime rate, me mateys?' asked Michael. He was playing the moderator. He only agreed to do the job on the grounds that he could do so dressed up as a pirate. So he was wearing an eye-patch and adding 'avast thee' or 'me matey' or a 'ye scurvy dogs' to all the questions.

'Is there a rising crime rate?' asked Nanny Piggins.

'I don't know,' admitted Michael, 'but that's a question they always ask in political debates so you'd better have an answer.'

'I think people should take more personal responsibility for their property,' said Nanny Piggins. 'You can't rely on the police to do everything for you. The Police Sergeant is a busy man. I'm forever needing his help to get out of scrapes. So he can't have his time wasted on trivial matters such as burglary and petty theft. If you've got nice things in your house and you don't want anyone to steal them, here's what you do . . .'

'Buy insurance?' guessed Derrick.

'What's insurance?' asked Nanny Piggins.

(I know it is extraordinary to think that a pig who was regularly blasted out of a military-grade cannon could have no idea what insurance was, but Nanny Piggins was so glamorous and charming that even though she often slammed into a pedestrian's head at 60 miles an hour, she had never been subject to a public liability claim.)

'Insurance is when you pay an annual amount to an insurance company, so that if something bad happens, for instance you get robbed or your house burns down, they will pay you lots of money to help replace things,' explained Derrick.

'That sounds an awful lot like gambling,' said Nanny Piggins.

Nanny Piggins was very prudish about

gambling because the Ringmaster had once bet that if he tampered with the trajectory of her cannon, he could blast her over the top of the Eiffel Tower. Of course Nanny Piggins had triumphantly sailed over the famous French landmark, but she was very cross to pass the Jules Verne restaurant at the top and not be able to stop for a slice of cake. She had been against gambling ever since.

'Insurance sounds like you are betting that something terrible will happen to you,' said Nanny Piggins.

The children realised Nanny Piggins was entirely right.

'No, I don't approve of that,' continued Nanny Piggins. 'I believe that if you don't want someone to steal from you, you should leave a large chocolate cake on your doorstep every night. Any thief would see the cake and stop to have a bite. After consuming one mouthful, they would find it impossible to resist the rest of the cake, and so would have to sit down and eat the whole thing. At which point they would be too full of food to do anything as athletic as climbing in through an upstairs bathroom window, and too grateful to the provider of the cake to ever dream of stealing from them.'

'But *you* don't do that,' pointed out Michael.

'Well, I don't need to, do I?' said Nanny Piggins. 'If anyone ever had the temerity to break in here (as one fool did – for more information read Chapter 8 of *The Adventures of Nanny Piggins*), they would not be sitting down to bite into a cake, I would be biting into their shins.'

'So you approve of vigilante violence?' accused Derrick in his role as Mayor Bloomsbridge.

'What's vigilante violence?' asked Nanny Piggins.

'It's where people take the law into their own hands,' explained Samantha.

'Oh, then yes, I certainly do,' agreed Nanny Piggins. 'I tremendously enjoy making citizens' arrests. It takes all my strength of character not to arrest my two opponents for crimes against fashion.'

'You're assuming that the mayor and Father will be wearing bad clothes to the debate,' said Samantha.

'I think that is a safe assumption,' agreed Nanny Piggins.

'What would you do about education, ye scurvy dogs?' asked Michael.

'Why would I want to do anything about that?' asked Nanny Piggins.

'Education is always a big election issue,' explained Samantha.

'Why?' asked Nanny Piggins. 'Because so many people want to abolish it?'

'No, the opposite. They always want the education system to be better so that their children will do better,' explained Samantha.

'But if everybody did better, then everybody would have to try harder and work more,' said Nanny Piggins. 'Surely it makes more sense just to carry on as we are now and let children relax a bit.'

'I think voters like schools to do more, and have more equipment,' explained Samantha.

'But if teachers were better equipped to teach, where would all that teaching go?' asked Nanny Piggins.

Derrick as the mayor just shook his head. He did not have an answer.

And as Mr Green was being played by an empty coat rack, he didn't have an answer either.

'They would shove the extra teaching into the children's heads,' continued Nanny Piggins, 'and who is going to make the children's heads bigger to accommodate this extra learning that they are supposed to be doing?'

'I don't think you can make a child's head bigger,' said Boris. 'Well, you probably could if you grabbed them by their ears and pulled them hard enough to stretch their skull a bit. But it would be tremendously painful.'

'And education is painful enough without yanking on children's skulls,' said Nanny Piggins. 'No, I don't approve of any additional education. The only adjustment to the school system I would make is to drop all the useless subjects like maths, geography and chemistry and replace them with cake baking. Cake baking includes maths, geography and chemistry but it is a much nicer way of learning about them.'

'Pish!' declared Derrick, in his role as the mayor (he had picked up some of Nanny Piggins' debating terminology).

'It's true,' declared Nanny Piggins. 'To make a good Dundee cake you must measure all the ingredients, which is maths, know that Dundee is in Scotland, which is geography, and combine the ingredients in the right way and at the right temperature to entirely change their physical structure, which is carbon chemistry. And the best bit about educating children through cake baking is that if their skulls do start to ache from all the knowledge going in there, they can sit down and eat a slice of cake to make themselves feel better.'

Boris broke into rapturous applause. 'There is no

way you can't win,' he said, mopping tears from his eyes. 'Your policies make so much sense. The only way you could miss out on being mayor is if someone higher up hears what you've got to say and insists you immediately take over the whole country instead.'

'I had considered that danger,' agreed Nanny Piggins. 'Rest assured I am ready to bite anyone on the shins who tries to get me to run for national office.'

'We'd better get going,' said Samantha, checking her watch. 'The debate is in two hours and they'll want you to be there an hour early so they can do your hair and make-up.'

'They'll do what?!' exclaimed Nanny Piggins.

'They always do your hair and make-up before you appear on television,' explained Samantha.

'How impertinent,' said Nanny Piggins. 'As if I would let some amateur interfere with my hair. They're not qualified.'

'I'm sure they use trained hairdressers,' said Michael.

'A trained hairdresser?' exclaimed Nanny Piggins. 'That's a contradiction in terms. My hair knows more about what to do with itself than any hairdresser would. I look perfectly fabulous as I am now!' – which was true – 'We shall set out now, but only so we can go to the sweet shop on the way to the studio to stock up on supplies. You will all need pockets full of lollies so that you don't fall asleep while your father is talking. And I shall need pockets full of lollies both for eating and for throwing at your father when I strongly disagree with his point, which I anticipate will be quite a lot, so I have worn a dress with extra-large pockets.'

The detour to the sweet shop took a full hour and a half and it was actually excellent debating practice, because they spent most of the time arguing which sweet would be optimal both for deliciousness and painfulness when thrown at an opponent's ear. Clearly anything light and fluffy like marshmallows or strawberry bonbons would not do. They needed a heavier sweet, perhaps a hardened caramel or a boiled lolly?

Eventually Nanny Piggins decided on a combination of chocolate éclairs and sherbet lemons (both were hard and heavy), with a side stash of extra-long chocolate bars either for eating or hitting her opponents over the head if they refused to concede she was right.

So they arrived at the television station ten minutes before the scheduled start of the debate and were greeted by a very anxious producer.

'You were supposed to be here an hour and a half ago,' the producer wailed.

'Get a grip of yourself, woman,' said Nanny Piggins, shoving a sherbet lemon into the producer's mouth in the hope that the sugar would help calm her down. 'Remember, this is only television. If I hadn't turned up, what is the worst that could have happened? You could show a re-run of *The Young and the Irritable* and the electorate would probably learn more. They would certainly be a lot better entertained.'

'If you hadn't turned up,' said the producer as she ushered them through security and into the building, 'things could have been much worse than that. The debate would have gone ahead with just Mayor Bloomsbridge and Mr Green.'

'But that would be the most dangerously boring hour of television ever broadcast,' protested Nanny Piggins.

'I know, that's why I'm so glad you're here,' said the producer.

While the receptionist took forever misspelling their names on their visitors' cards, Nanny Piggins, Boris and the children took a moment to look about the television station. The debate was being filmed at the proper television station in the city and it was much more impressive than their local community television station. True, the building was still run-down – it needed a paint job and the halls were lined with faded photos of celebrities who hadn't been famous for thirty years – but it was a big building with a lift, so it had a much more professional feel.'

'Where's the outfit you'll be wearing?' asked the producer.

Nanny Piggins glowered.

'You shouldn't have said that,' muttered Derrick.

'What . . .' asked Nanny Piggins, glaring hard, 'is wrong with what I have on?'

'Say "nothing, you look fabulous",' urged Michael.

'Um,' said the producer, 'it's just that you are wearing a floor-length, crimson designer evening gown and usually politicians wear grey suits.'

'Further evidence that they are fools,' said Nanny Piggins. 'If they have not got the panache to look traffic-stoppingly fabulous, then that is their problem. I am a trained circus pig. Looking good, often while travelling at supersonic speeds through the air, is my speciality.'

At this point they only had six minutes until the broadcast started, so the producer decided to avoid any further discussion and quickly usher Nanny Piggins into the lift.

'Are you nervous?' asked Derrick.

'About what?' asked Nanny Piggins.

'Being on television in front of millions of people,' said Derrick.

'Piffle!' exclaimed Nanny Piggins. 'It is the viewers who should be nervous about what they're about to witness.'

Suddenly the lift lurched to a halt.

'What was that?' asked Samantha.

The producer pressed the tenth-floor button on the panel over and over.

'Unless that button generates energy through you repeatedly pressing it, I don't see how what you're doing is of any use,' said Nanny Piggins.

'The broadcast starts in three minutes,' panicked the producer. 'We don't have time to be stuck in a lift.'

'Why don't you try the emergency button?' suggested Boris. 'I always wanted to have an emergency in a lift so I could press that button.'

The producer pressed the emergency button, and in the distance they could hear an alarm bell ring.

'That just sounds like a loud doorbell,' said Nanny Piggins. 'If no-one does anything when a car alarm goes off, they are hardly going to leap into action because they hear a loud doorbell.'

'Try the telephone,' urged Boris. 'The secret one behind the panel. I've always wanted to use that too.'

'You use that all the time,' chided Michael.

'Well, sometimes in a lift I get lonely,' explained Boris, 'so I like to ring up the lift mechanics and have a little chat.'

The producer picked up the phone and held it to her ear. 'It's dead!' she wailed.

'Of course it is,' said Nanny Piggins. 'It's an inanimate object.'

'No, I mean the line is dead,' said the producer. 'There's no dial tone.'

'Perhaps it's because someone has cut that big wire,' pointed out Michael.

They looked down to see that the handset was entirely detached from the base unit. The cord had clearly been hacked in two by a blunt pair of scissors.

'I am beginning to suspect sabotage,' said Nanny Piggins.

'You think someone did this on purpose?' asked the producer.

'Of course,' said Nanny Piggins.

'But who would do such a thing?' asked the producer.

'We must ask, who stands to gain from my being trapped in a lift two minutes before the mayoral debate is about to begin?' said Nanny Piggins.

'Father,' exclaimed Samantha.

'And Mayor Bloomsbridge,' said Derrick.

'Precisely,' said Nanny Piggins. 'That one of them was capable of something as imaginative as this actually raises them in my estimation. Nonetheless, I shall have to escape and punish them as a matter of principle.'

'But how?' asked the producer. 'We're six storeys up. You can't climb about in the lift shaft when we're this far off the ground.'

Nanny Piggins just laughed.

'Nanny Piggins is the world's greatest flying pig,' Derrick explained. 'She can do things six storeys up that most people can't even do on the ground.'

'But you're wearing a floor-length, designer evening gown,' said the producer.

'We'll soon change that,' said Nanny Piggins. She undid the zip and stepped out of her dress. This was nowhere near as shocking as it sounds because, naturally, Nanny Piggins had worn her hot-pink wrestling leotard underneath.

'Nanny Piggins!' exclaimed Derrick. 'Why were you wearing your wrestling leotard under your dress?'

'I thought it would be best to prepare for all eventualities,' said Nanny Piggins evasively.

'You were planning to end the debate by putting Father and Mayor Bloomsbridge in a painful leg lock, weren't you,' accused Derrick.

'Perhaps,' said Nanny Piggins. 'I thought it would be a good way to demonstrate my ability to get things done.'

'The debate is starting in 60 seconds,' urged the producer. 'If you're going to get us out of here, you need to do something now!'

'No problem,' said Nanny Piggins. 'Boris, would you be a dear and smash me feet first into that service hatch in the ceiling so I can kick it open?'

'All right,' said Boris as he spun his sister upside down and rammed her into the ceiling.

'Ow!' yelled Nanny Piggins, which made Boris drop her (on her head) and burst into tears.

'Ow!' she said again as she landed on the floor.

'What's wrong?' asked Samantha as they crouched around to check that their nanny was all right.

'I've broken my sister's ankles!' wept Boris.

'I'm fine,' said Nanny Piggins. 'Stop weeping, Boris. A slight double sprain is all. I've never had any trouble kicking open a lift service hatch before. I suspect foul play.'

'When have you had to kick open a lift service hatch before?' asked Michael.

'Oh, many, many times,' said Nanny Piggins. 'The Ringmaster is always coming up with new and imaginative ways to kidnap me and sometimes they do involve lift shafts. Service hatches are designed to be easily opened in an emergency so this one must have been tampered with, possibly with superglue.'

'What are we going to do?' asked Samantha. 'Does that mean we are trapped – forever?!' She started to hyperventilate.

'Pull yourself together,' said Nanny Piggins. 'This is a confined space. Only one of us can go into hysterics at a time and Boris has already gone first. You have to wait your turn. Here, have a bag of sherbet lemons. It will take your mind off things.'

Samantha gratefully started sucking on her sherbet lemon. They were her all-time favourite sweet. If she was going to spend the rest of her life in a lift shaft, she was glad that this was the food she would be trapped with.

'If the service hatch is sealed shut,' continued Nanny Piggins, 'we will just have to make another service hatch.'

'How?' asked Derrick.

'Fortunately we have been trapped in the lift with a ten-foot-tall Kodiak bear in supreme athletic condition,' said Nanny Piggins. 'Boris, I want you to stop crying and punch a hole in the roof please.'

'I can't,' sobbed Boris.

'If you don't, we'll run out of oxygen in about seven minutes,' said Nanny Piggins.

Without hesitating, Boris used every ounce of his strength to slam an uppercut into the ceiling panels, tearing aside the insulation and sheet metal and making a neat hole up into the shaft.

'Thank you, Boris,' said Nanny Piggins kindly. 'Now if you'll just rip the sides of the hole so that it is a bit bigger, you can go back to having your hysterics.'

'Thank you,' said Boris as he quickly tore the opening wider, then sat down on the floor and dissolved into wracking sobs.

Nanny Piggins climbed up Boris, stood on tippy-toes on top of his head (which was not easy given that he was sobbing and therefore shuddering back and forth), then pulled herself up through the hole and into the darkness of the lift shaft.

'What can you see?' asked Derrick.

'Nothing,' said Nanny Piggins. 'It's pitch-black.

Lift shafts aren't at all like they are in action movies. There is no internal lighting and no-one thought of putting in any windows.'

'What are you going to do?' asked Michael.

'I suppose I could light a fire,' pondered Nanny Piggins.

'No!' yelled everyone in the lift in unison.

'All right,' said Nanny Piggins. 'I know, I'll just smell my way.'

'What does she mean?' asked the producer.

'Nanny Piggins has an extraordinary sense of smell,' explained Derrick.

'She can smell things other people can't,' added Michael.

'Like a chocolate truck travelling at full speed one hundred kilometres away,' added Samantha.

'Or how many cakes you could buy with the amount of money you have in your wallet,' added Michael.

'Surely not?' asked the producer.

'I can smell that you have a five-dollar note and two twenty-cent pieces in your pocket,' called Nanny Piggins. 'That would buy you one slice of mud cake and half a doughnut from Hans' Bakery.'

'You see,' said Michael.

'Okay, I've found the lift cable,' called Nanny

Piggins. 'I'm going to shinny up that until I get to the floor where the debate is being held.'

'How will you smell for that?' asked Derrick.

'I'll sniff for pomposity,' said Nanny Piggins. 'Your father always has a heavy odour of it about him, and the mayor is even worse.'

They listened to Nanny Piggins climb the lift cable. Which was not a very loud noise because she was such an expert climber of cabling. You have to be when you are a circus performer because the Ringmaster would sometimes try to hide from her by climbing up to the top of the Big Top tent, so naturally Nanny Piggins would have to shinny up the guy ropes to give his shins the good biting they deserved.

'I don't know why they have to put so much thick grease on the cables,' complained Nanny Piggins. 'It's going to be devilishly hard to get off my hot-pink wrestling leotard. It was bad enough getting the chocolate stain out that time I wrestled the profiterole out of Headmaster Pimplestock's hand because I felt anyone who stocked generic health food bars in the school canteen did not deserve a chocolate treat themselves.'

'I suppose they have to put grease on the cables so that the lift can go up and down,' said Michael.

'Well, it's very inconvenient to people like me who have to climb up here and dramatically save the day,' said Nanny Piggins. 'Hang on –' they could hear Nanny Piggins sniffing – 'I think I'm at the right floor, I can smell your father's socks. He's been wearing the same ones for three weeks because he is too lazy to wash them and too cheap to throw them away.'

'How are you going to get the door open?' asked Derrick.

'I don't know,' admitted Nanny Piggins. 'I left my crowbar in my other leotard. Boris, I don't suppose you could climb up here and wrench these doors open for me?'

Boris didn't answer with words, he just wept louder (and being Russian, he had already been weeping very loudly to begin with).

Nanny Piggins sighed. 'If you do come up here and help me,' she continued, 'I'll give you a honey sandwich.'

Boris leapt to his feet and somehow pulled his considerable frame through the petite pig-sized hole, all in less than a millisecond. He was soon scrambling up the cabling to meet his sister.

'Stand aside,' he ordered urgently.

'I can't stand aside,' said Nanny Piggins. 'I'm hanging on a lift cable.'

'Then stand on my head,' said Boris, 'so I can get this door open.'

Nanny Piggins evidently did as she was instructed because soon a beam of light shone into the lift shaft where Boris had used his considerable strength to wrench the lift door open.

'Honey sandwich?' he asked hopefully.

Nanny Piggins reached into her hot-pink wrestling leotard and pulled out a snap-lock bag containing a (slightly squashed) honey sandwich. She always carried one about her person, just in case she had a motivational emergency with Boris.

Boris grabbed the bag (he found it hard to act like a gentleman in the presence of honey) and swallowed it whole. 'Mmm, delicious,' he said.

'How do you know?' asked Nanny Piggins. 'You didn't even take the sandwich out of the plastic bag!'

'My stomach knows,' said Boris, 'and it is grateful I didn't waste any time with unwrapping.'

'Now we'd better rescue the others,' said Nanny Piggins.

'Don't waste time!' urged the producer from down in the lift shaft. 'Go and join in the debate!'

Nanny Piggins peered down into the darkness.

'That is the difference between you, a TV producer, and me, a normal, morally balanced pig,' said Nanny

Piggins. 'You think it is more important that I go and contribute to some mundane television program that everyone will forget as soon as it is over. Whereas I think it is more important to rescue three children, and you, from being trapped inside a lift shaft.'

'You can rescue us later,' cried the TV producer.

'It's sad really,' said Nanny Piggins conversationally to her brother. 'Everyone in television has Stockholm Syndrome regarding their job. What sort of mayoral candidate would leave a seven-year-old, a nine-year-old, an eleven-year-old and a very silly grown woman stuck in a lift shaft just so they could appear on television.'

'A winning one,' argued the producer.

'Derrick, give that woman a chocolate bar,' called Nanny Piggins. 'She's talking absolute rubbish and I'm sick of listening to it.'

'How are we going to get them up?' asked Boris.

'I was thinking we could put a whole heap of explosives at the bottom of the lift shaft and blow the lift right out of the building,' suggested Nanny Piggins.

'Do we have any explosives in the car?' asked Boris.

'No,' conceded Nanny Piggins. 'I took them all out so we could get more cake in the boot.'

'How about I just pull the lift up, hand over hand, using the lift cable?' suggested Boris.

'Do you think you could?' asked Nanny Piggins.

'Oh yes,' said Boris, 'if I did it quickly, while the honey sandwich in my stomach is still giving me lots of energy.'

And so that is what they did. Boris pulled up the lift until Nanny Piggins could reach down through their improvised service hatch and pull the children out one at a time. Nanny Piggins even pulled the producer out, although she did seriously consider leaving her there in the dark, stuck in a lonely lift shaft – to give her the opportunity to rethink her sordid profession.

'Where's this debate then?' asked Nanny Piggins.

'Through the big double doors,' said the producer.

'Let's get stuck into some political discourse,' said Nanny Piggins with a menacing gleam in her eye.

She strode forward and kicked open the double doors, which wasn't the most sensible thing to do because they were swinging doors, so they immediately swung back at her. Fortunately Nanny Piggins was a gifted athlete so she deftly stepped forward, allowing the doors to swing back and hit the producer on the nose.

'Right,' said Nanny Piggins, pointing her trotter at Mr Green and Mayor Bloomsbridge. 'Which one of you naughty men is responsible for me being trapped in the lift?'

The audience was riveted. Several of them had fallen asleep during the long, boring and pompous monologues each candidate had already indulged in, and the ones who had not fallen asleep desperately wished they could, or fall unconscious, or astral-project their minds to a parallel universe. So they were delighted to see a grease-smeared pig in a hot-pink wrestling leotard burst into the studio and start yelling.

'It wasn't me!' protested Mayor Bloomsbridge.

'Don't think your lack of initiative wins you any favours with me,' declared Nanny Piggins. 'I fully intend to give you a good hard bite on the shins because I'm just that annoyed.'

'It wasn't me either,' protested Mr Green, a lot less convincingly. 'I didn't do it. You can't prove I bribed the lift technician. There is no evidence that will stand up against me in a court of law.'

'I have no intention of taking this matter to a court of law,' said Nanny Piggins in an ominously low whisper. 'I'm going to take this matter to the court of my foot, which I shall soon be planting on your bottom for being such a disgraceful man.'

'Someone stop her!' pleaded Mr Green as he ran and tried to hide behind the debate moderator. This only did further damage to his campaign, because in reality the moderator was a heavily pregnant woman (not a pirate), and Mr Green using her as a human shield was not a pretty image for the television news bulletin.

'How dare you tamper with the lift to trap us in a dark lift shaft just so you could blather on here in front of the cameras,' accused Nanny Piggins. 'I can understand you doing it to me. But your own children?! Have you no sense of decency?'

'I'm a tax lawyer,' said Mr Green. 'They train us not to.'

What followed was an extremely exciting half hour of television. First of all Nanny Piggins chased Mr Green and Mayor Bloomsbridge around and around the studio, and then there was a lot of wrestling, some begging for mercy and a good long telling off. The audience enjoyed every moment of it. They unanimously agreed that Nanny Piggins was the clear winner of the debate. Even her policies impressed them. But then political policies do sound more impressive when you yell them at a political rival while sitting on him and giving him a wet willy.

'Thank you, thank you, thank you,' said the producer as she escorted Nanny Piggins, Boris and the children back to their car.

'What for? For rescuing you from the lift?' asked Nanny Piggins.

'Oh yes, that was very kind of you,' agreed the producer, 'but thank you for making some really great television.'

'You do realise that the future leadership of our town is at stake too, don't you?' asked Nanny Piggins.

'Oh yes, and of course that's important as well,' agreed the producer.

'Did you enjoy the debate?' asked Derrick as they drove home.

'Oh yes,' said Nanny Piggins. 'Secretly, I'm even grateful to Mr Green for trapping me in the lift shaft. It meant I got to avoid all that boring talking they did at the beginning and just sweep in for the fun wrestling bit at the end.'

'You know, political debates don't normally include wrestling,' said Derrick.

'Really?!' said Nanny Piggins, genuinely surprised. 'They jolly well should. It's the best bit as far as I can see. I think it humanises the candidates to see their faces squashed into a linoleum floor.'

## CHAPTER 9

### *Nanny Piggins and the Hidden Treasure*

Derrick, Samantha and Michael were having a very dull Saturday. For the first time since Nanny Piggins had become their nanny, they were teetering on the edge of having absolutely nothing to do because at 8 o'clock that morning, Nanny Piggins had left the house to join a roadside litter picking-up crew as a photo opportunity for her mayoral campaign.

Nanny Piggins was not trying to make a point about the deplorable amount of litter on their local roads under the current mayor's administration. She was trying to make a point about local petty criminals who were forced to spend their weekends picking it up. She thought it was a terrible waste of their time.

'Burglars, petty thieves and vandals have much better things to do,' argued Nanny Piggins. 'The burglars are good at breaking into things so they could spend their time helping people who have locked themselves out of their homes or cars. And instead of paying for roadside signs, the council could just get the vandals to spray important civic messages like "Don't forget to wear a seatbelt" and "Please don't run anybody over with your car".'

'But who would pick up the rubbish then?' asked Derrick.

'All the useless people who wouldn't be missed elsewhere,' said Nanny Piggins. 'Headmaster Pimplestock for a start. I'm sure the school would run much more efficiently without him. Then if you round up all the insurance salesmen and lawyers, and maths teachers – give them a pointy stick and a sack and they could finally do an honest day's work.'

Normally Nanny Piggins would have taken the children with her. She found that even the most tedious occasions could end up being educational, especially if you released a rat or threw someone in a swamp. But on this occasion the children were not allowed to join her, because of the occupational health and safety rules – you had to be over 18 to pick up rubbish. Nanny Piggins was all for dyeing their hair grey and setting them up with fake moustaches, but the children thought it better if she waited until she was mayor before she started flagrantly disobeying council regulations.

And so it was 10.53 in the morning. Derrick, Samantha and Michael had done all their homework, tidied their rooms, whipped up a chocolate cake to cheer up their nanny when she eventually got home, and now they were at a loss as to what to do with themselves.

'What would Nanny Piggins want us to do?' asked Michael.

'Go frog catching?' guessed Samantha.

'Drop something off the roof?' guessed Derrick.

'She'd probably want us to go and rescue her from picking up rubbish,' guessed Boris.

All four of them sighed simultaneously.

'What did we used to do on Saturdays before Nanny Piggins was around?' asked Samantha.

'We had empty meaningless lives,' said Derrick.

They all sighed again.

Saturday became much more interesting when Nanny Piggins burst in through the back door.

'Thank goodness you're all here!' she exclaimed.

Nanny Piggins looked quite a sight. Her hair was messy. Her clothes were grubby. And she actually looked like she had been sweating. (And sweating was something she usually never did because she deeply resented the expression 'sweating like a pig'.) But most shockingly of all, she was wearing a bright orange iridescent vest that did not go with her lavender frock at all.

'Sarah!' exclaimed Boris. 'What are you wearing?'

'What?' said Nanny Piggins, before looking down and noticing the hideous glowing vest. 'Oh yes, they made me wear it. They said it was so cars wouldn't hit me. But I said I would rather be hit by a car than look so awful.'

'You poor thing,' said Boris, clutching his sister to his chest in a big bear hug.

'Actually it wasn't too bad,' said Nanny Piggins. 'They gave us each a garbage bag and a long stick with a nail in it. We were supposed to use the stick to pick up litter but I found it was equally good for poking the supervisor in the bottom when she looked the other way.'

'You didn't!' exclaimed Samantha.

'Oh yes I did,' said Nanny Piggins. 'I thought if she was going to ruin everyone's Saturday morning by making them pick up litter, then I would ruin her afternoon by making her get a tetanus injection.'

'So you had a bad time?' asked Derrick.

'On the contrary, picking up litter was wonderful!' exclaimed Nanny Piggins. 'We should do it sometime. It's tremendous fun. It is amazing what people throw out of their car windows. Sure, there are lots of useless things like food wrappers, mobile phones and country and western CDs. And they do sometimes purposefully throw them at your head. But that only makes the job more exciting, because it is quite a challenge to catch a half-eaten hamburger and throw it back at the same car it came from. I was much better at it than any of the other community servers and we had a professional cricket player in our group. But sometimes people throw really good things out of their cars.'

'Like what?' asked Derrick doubtfully.

'Like half-eaten cake,' said Nanny Piggins. 'One driver threw a delicious lemon tart right into my open mouth.'

'No!' exclaimed Michael disbelievingly.

'All right, I did have to run fifty metres and leap up in the air to catch it in my open mouth, but that's definitely where it landed,' clarified Nanny Piggins.

'That doesn't sound very hygienic,' worried Samantha.

'It's all right, I didn't touch it with my hands,' Nanny Piggins assured her. 'But that's not the best bit. That's not the reason why I'm home early.'

'Yes, I was wondering about that,' said Samantha. 'You said you wouldn't be home until 6 o'clock.'

'I know,' said Nanny Piggins, 'but I just had to tie the supervisor to a bush and run off right away, as soon as I found this.'

Nanny Piggins took a sheet of folded paper out of her pocket and laid it on the table. The paper looked old and worn around the edges – more cloth-like than paper-like. And as she unfolded it they could all see an array of strange drawings and notations.

'What is it?' asked Michael.

'A treasure map!' exclaimed Nanny Piggins.

'You found a treasure map on the side of the road?' asked Derrick, again doubtfully.

'Perhaps a pirate threw it out of his window as he drove past,' guessed Nanny Piggins.

'It looks like it's a map of our town,' said Derrick. 'An old map before there were any buildings.'

'Exactly, from the olden pirate days,' agreed Nanny Piggins.

'How could an olden days pirate throw this out of a car window?' asked Samantha. 'Pirates haven't been around for hundreds of years.'

'Perhaps he left instructions in his will for his great-great-great grandson to throw it out of a car window?' suggested Nanny Piggins.

'But how would he have known cars were going to be invented?' asked Michael.

'He must have been a very clever pirate,' said Nanny Piggins.

'Look, there's an X!' said Derrick as he peered closely at the map.

'Yes, I saw that,' said Nanny Piggins. 'The map maker must have made a spelling mistake there and had to cross it out.'

'No, X marks the spot,' explained Derrick. 'That's where the treasure must be.'

'Really?' said Nanny Piggins. 'It's as simple as that? I thought there would be invisible ink, or a riddle to solve, or something.'

'We could find some riddles to solve if you like,' said Michael.

'No thank you,' said Nanny Piggins. 'I don't really care for riddles. I can never think of the answer because I'm too busy thinking about biting the person for asking such a silly question in the first place.'

Nanny Piggins rolled the map back up and tucked it inside her iridescent vest. 'All right, gather up all the essential supplies. We'll be heading out to find the pirate treasure and untold riches in five minutes.'

'What essential supplies?' asked Michael.

'All the cake we can carry, of course,' said Nanny Piggins. 'Treasure hunting is sure to be hungry work.'

'Shouldn't we take a compass?' asked Michael.

'You can if you like,' said Nanny Piggins, 'but I don't see that there's any need to. I always know exactly which way is which. The Slimbridge Cake Factory is south. Hans' Bakery is west. Mrs Hesselstein's Chocolatorium is east. And Santa's house is north. So you can tell which way is which just by sniffing the air.'

'What does Santa's house smell like?' asked Samantha. (Her own nose was not capable of sensing one dwelling in the Arctic Circle.)

'Peppermint sticks,' said Nanny Piggins, 'and reindeer poop. He really should get the elves to muck out the stable more frequently.'

Just then there was a loud knock at the door.

BANG! BANG! BANG!

'Nanny Piggins, we know you're in there, we can see your muddy trotter prints going down the side of the house,' called the Police Sergeant. 'Please come out. If you come back to the litter collection team right away and say you're sorry, the supervisor isn't going to press charges.'

'The poor Police Sergeant, he's such a sweetie,' said Nanny Piggins. 'Remind me to bake him a batch of jim-jams when all this is over.'

'But his favourite is shortbread biscuits,' argued Samantha.

'I know,' said Nanny Piggins, 'but he really needs to broaden his horizons. Man cannot live by shortbread alone. Although I believe several Scottish people have had fun trying.'

'I'm going to give you to the count of ten and then I'm going to have to kick the door in,' warned the Police Sergeant. 'I really don't want to damage your lock, or my foot, so I would really appreciate it if you would open up. One . . .'

'Quick!' said Nanny Piggins. 'There's no time for supplies. Everybody, out the window!'

Nanny Piggins leapt out the open kitchen window.

'Why can't we go out the back door?' asked Derrick.

'Probably because it's not as much fun,' guessed Michael as he clambered up on the kitchen sink and followed his nanny.

A short time later they were sneaking down the back alley behind their house. Nanny Piggins had disguised herself as a wisteria bush (the flowers looked lovely with her dress). Although, while they did entirely cover her face, she had neglected to obscure the iridescent vest.

Fortunately, however, the Police Constable had hurt his foot when he kicked in the front door, so the Police Sergeant had to take him to hospital, which bought them some time.

And so just a few short hours later, by using the still existing geographical features of the map and Nanny Piggins' unique nasal compass, they found themselves on the edge of town, standing outside the gates of Dulsford Estate.

'The treasure is in there,' declared Nanny Piggins, checking the map, then sniffing the air just to be sure. 'Yes, nor-north east of the bend in the river. And . . .' she sniffed the air again, 'four miles to the east of Hans' bakery.'

'But we can't get in there,' protested Derrick. 'Mr Dulsford, the richest man in Dulsford, lives there.'

'Plus those walls must be at least 25 feet high,' added Michael.

'It's very antisocial,' complained Boris. 'I'm not used to finding walls I can't peek over. It makes me suspect they must have vast vats of honey on the other side. Why else would they go to so much trouble to make their wall bearproof?'

'Pish to that!' said Nanny Piggins. 'I'm the world's greatest flying pig. I'm not going to let a little thing like a 25 foot stone wall stop me.'

'I think there is broken glass cemented to the top of it,' warned Michael.

'I'm going to get over it without even touching the top,' declared Nanny Piggins. 'Just you watch.'

Nanny Piggins disappeared into the nearby woods. After a few moments they could hear the sound of leaves rustling, as Nanny Piggins climbed a tree; then they heard the sound of a great big branch being ripped off that tree. Nanny Piggins emerged from the woods a few seconds later dragging a huge leafy branch.

'What are you going to do with that?' asked Derrick.

'Are you going to disguise yourself as a Trojan Tree,' guessed Boris, 'and leave yourself outside the gates in the hope that Mr Dulsford is a great tree lover who will take you inside, where you can leap out and attack him?'

'No, although that would have been a jolly good plan too,' conceded Nanny Piggins. 'No, I've got an even better idea. Just watch.'

Nanny Piggins took out her nail file and began whittling. It was quite an astonishing display. There are machines at lumber yards that cannot strip a tree as quickly as Nanny Piggins with a nail file. Within a few short minutes she had reduced the big bushy branch to one long pole.

'Are you going to use that to poke Mr Dulsford through the slates in the gate?' guessed Boris.

'No,' said Nanny Piggins, 'at least not at first. I may try that if this doesn't work. I'm going to use this long stick to pole-vault over the wall.'

'But the world record for pole-vault is 20.177 feet,' protested Derrick, 'and that's with a proper fibre-glass pole.'

'World record by who?' demanded Nanny Piggins.

'Serge Bubka of the Ukraine,' supplied Derrick.

'Ah, you mean a human,' said Nanny Piggins. 'Well, of course he didn't get very high. All those human disadvantages: great long legs dangling in the way, skinny unaerodynamic body, and I bet he didn't have six chocolate mud cakes and half a lemon tart for breakfast.'

'You know what you're doing, don't you?' worried Samantha.

'Of course,' said Nanny Piggins. 'I've seen it on television. You remember that time the remote control got lost and the TV was stuck on the sports channel for three days before we discovered that I had accidentally baked it into a fruit cake?'

'If only you had baked it into a chocolate cake, you would have found it much sooner,' sighed Boris.

'Which is another reason why you should never ever bake fruit cake,' agreed Nanny Piggins.

Nanny Piggins picked up her pole and dragged it back to the far side of the street, getting ready for her run-up.

'Shouldn't you do some warm-up exercises?' asked Samantha.

'Or at least get one of us to hold your handbag for you?' suggested Michael.

'Stop fussing,' said Nanny Piggins. 'I need to concentrate now.'

Nanny Piggins picked up the pole and glared hard at the wall. To give her credit, when Nanny Piggins tried her hand at a new athletic event she seemed to master it effortlessly every time. Watching her take several deep breaths while beginning to rock back and forth with her pole lifted at just the right angle from the ground – Nanny Piggins did indeed look exactly like an Olympic athlete on the television.

Suddenly she burst forward, and despite having extremely short legs (extremely short everything because she was only four feet tall), Nanny Piggins could turn on an incredible burst of speed. She was a blur of movement as she streaked towards the wall, planted her pole firmly and hoisted herself up, swinging high into the air.

'Yiiiiipeeeeee!' cried Nanny Piggins as she easily arced 25 feet off the ground, flying towards the clear sky above the wall. That was until something terrible happened. In less than a millisecond a siren went off and a perspex bandit screen (like they have in banks) flew up, adding another 6 feet to the wall. Nanny Piggins slammed straight into the centre of a perspex panel, then slid all the way down the wall before landing hard on her bottom.

'Are you all right, Nanny Piggins?' called Samantha as they all rushed forward to check on her.

'I'm okay,' said Nanny Piggins a little groggily,
'although I think I may have broken my chocolate
bar.'

Nanny Piggins took a chocolate bar out of her
back pocket. Mercifully it was still intact so she ate it
before any further harm could come to it.

'Perhaps we should go home now,' suggested
Samantha.

'Pish!' said Nanny Piggins. 'We'll just have to
come up with another plan.'

'Could it be a plan to have honey sandwiches on
a picnic rug down by the river?' asked Boris optimis-
tically. He loved honey sandwiches and picnic honey
sandwiches were the best kind of honey sandwiches
of all.

'No, a plan to get over the wall,' said Nanny
Piggins. 'I know! Boris, you'll just have to throw me
over.'

'I can't do that,' protested Boris.

'Of course you can, you used to be the circus'
discus champion every year,' said Nanny Piggins.

'Yes, but that's because I used to imagine that
the discus was a rhubarb pie,' said Boris. 'I don't like
rhubarb pie. It's too rhubarby for my taste.'

'Well, just imagine I'm a rhubarb pie. Grab me by the trotters and hurl me over,' ordered Nanny Piggins.

'You don't look like a rhubarb pie,' said Boris.

'Close your eyes and imagine one,' suggested Nanny Piggins.

'All right,' conceded Boris, 'but I just want you to know that you are my sister and I love you and I wouldn't normally throw you 31 feet in the air unless you specifically asked me to and I thought you looked like a rhubarb pie.'

'Of course,' said Nanny Piggins.

And so the three horrified children stood and watched as Boris picked up their nanny and spun around and around in circles, building up speed before releasing her into the air. He got the speed and the height right, but all the spinning around made him dizzy and he threw Nanny Piggins in completely the wrong direction, right into the middle of the forest.

When they tried again, and Boris concentrated not just on throwing away the rhubarb pie, but throwing it over the wall, he was successful. Nanny Piggins flew over the wall and the bandit screen.

'We did it!' screamed Nanny Piggins triumphantly as she flew through the air. Unfortunately her triumph was again short-lived, because as soon as she passed over the wall, sirens went off, lights started flashing and somewhere in the distance an air raid siren began to wail.

'Okay,' called Nanny Piggins from the far side of the wall, where she had landed safely. 'Now throw the children over.'

'What?!' exclaimed the children in horror.

'Don't worry,' called Nanny Piggins. 'The ground is higher on this side. It's only a 24 foot drop for the landing.'

'I don't want to be thrown over,' panicked Samantha.

'I don't want to throw you over,' panicked Boris. 'You don't look anything like a rhubarb pie. Besides, I've just remembered rhubarb pie can be quite nice if you serve it with a really good egg custard and lots of extra honey.'

'It's okay,' called Nanny Piggins from an unexpected direction.

They turned to see her leaning out from the now open gate, just 50 metres down the road.

'I've found the switch for the gate,' she explained. 'Come on, you'd better hurry up before it shuts again.'

Derrick, Samantha and Michael scrambled after her. As much as they admired Nanny Piggins, none of them wanted to become 'The World's Greatest Flying Children'.

Once inside the gate, the siren seemed much louder, echoing off the long high wall.

'I don't like this,' said Samantha. 'We're going to be arrested for breaking and entering.'

'We haven't broken anything,' disagreed Nanny Piggins, 'and we are following a treasure map. There are laws saying you can follow a treasure map wherever it goes.'

'Are there?' asked Michael.

'Well, if there aren't, there should be,' said Nanny Piggins. 'It'll be the first thing I see to when I become mayor.'

'Which way do we have to go?' asked Derrick, desperate to get moving before they could be attacked by trained dogs, or worse, trained snipers.

Nanny Piggins consulted the map. 'The quickest way is through the bog of quicksand, across the rickety bridge and over the tumbling stream.'

'What?!' exclaimed Samantha, who was now seriously considering having a full hysterical attack on the ground.

'Don't worry,' said Nanny Piggins. 'This map is hundreds of years old. I'm sure the quicksand has been filled in and the tumbling stream has dried up due to global warming.'

Unfortunately Nanny Piggins could not have been more incorrect. There was definitely a bog of quicksand. Nanny Piggins easily ran across and the children were able to dodge around the worst bits and wade through the others without much trouble. But a 700-kilogram bear in a bog of quicksand is never going to do well. In the end, Nanny Piggins had to make a stretcher out of water reeds so they could all drag Boris through. (She refused to let him run around it. She did not want to be defeatist.)

Then they came to the rickety bridge over the tumbling stream. For a start, to call it a tumbling stream was a gross understatement. A more accurate term would have been a raging river. And the rickety bridge would have been better described as a few pieces of tangled string. Boris just sat down and wept.

'Why on earth would Mr Dulsford keep such dangerous things in his garden?' wondered Samantha.

'Perhaps so he can have things to do with his unpleasant relatives when they come to visit,' guessed Nanny Piggins. 'Maybe if I climb this tree I'll be able to figure out some way to rig up a flying fox.'

'What with?' asked Derrick.

'Perhaps a real fox!' said Nanny Piggins, ever the optimist.

But as she leapt up and grabbed the first branch, the strangest thing happened. The branch clicked down, revealing that it was really a lever. Then the entire 30 metre high tree bent over the river, and the trunk folded out to form a flat platform. 'A secret bridge!' exclaimed Nanny Piggins.

'Those pirates must have been very advanced for their time with their knowledge of electrical engineering,' said Michael.

'Come on, let's get the treasure,' said Nanny Piggins.

They all ran across the bridge, except for Boris. He had to be dragged still weeping because he was worried about getting his paws wet.

'There it is, up ahead!' said Nanny Piggins, pointing towards the opening of a cave. 'According to the map the treasure is buried in the Cave of Great Despair.'

'That doesn't sound like a very happy cave,' sniffed Boris. 'Couldn't we just have a picnic on the riverbank instead?'

'No, we can't,' said Derrick, behind them. 'Look! It's Mr Dulsford!'

The others all looked around to see a very elderly man speeding towards them on a quad bike with a pack of vicious-looking dogs running ahead.

'Oh dear,' said Samantha. 'Crazed dogs.'

'Oh dear,' said Boris. 'Crazed old man.'

'Come on, we've no time to lose,' said Nanny Piggins. 'Perhaps they will have buried some pirate swords with the pirate treasure and we can use that to fight them off.'

Nanny Piggins disappeared into the long winding tunnel and the others, not wanting to be too far away from their best source of protection (the crazed pig with an eighth dan blackbelt in Taekwondo), disappeared after her.

Fortunately Nanny Piggins had brought her miner's headlamp with her. She often carried it, just in case she stumbled across King Solomon's Chocolate Mine (a legendary underground abundance of naturally occurring chocolate that all pigs believed in).

'There it is! Look! 'X' marks the spot!' said Nanny Piggins triumphantly. And there was indeed a large X marked on the ground in neatly aligned stones.

'That's odd,' said Derrick. 'Pirates don't usually literally put an X on the ground. It's not very secret. The X is just supposed to be on the map.'

'Perhaps they were very considerate pirates,' suggested Nanny Piggins. 'They knew in the future that we would not be very good at map reading due to an over-dependence on GPS technology.'

Suddenly their conversation was interrupted as the wild dogs burst into the far end of the tunnel. The barks were deafeningly loud as they echoed about inside the enclosed space.

'We're doomed!' shrieked Samantha, which is something she had often thought but this was the first occasion when she'd had genuine cause to say it aloud.

'Pish!' said Nanny Piggins. 'Boris is very good with dogs. He knows how to talk to them. You'll take care of it won't you, dear.'

'Of course,' said Boris. 'I don't have anything against dogs personally but they really do need to learn a manners lesson, making all that noise.'

Boris drew himself up to his full height (which was actually ten and a half feet when he stood up straight and on his tippy-toes), stretched out his arms wide and then, just as the dogs came streaming around the corner and all caught sight of him, Boris bellowed the most terrifying roar: 'GGGGR-RRRRRRAAAAAAGGGGHHHHHH!'

The dogs slid to a stop on the dirt floor and scrambled off desperately in the opposite direction, whining with fear.

The children were frozen with fear themselves. They had never known their dear and sensitive friend to sound so terrifying.

'I do hate having to raise my voice,' said Boris, 'but with some animals it is the only way to communicate.'

The children all made a mental note not to hesitate next time Boris asked them to pass the honey pot.

'I've found it!' yelled Nanny Piggins.

The children turned. While they had been watching Boris' confrontation with the dogs, Nanny Piggins had made an impressive start on the digging. She had disappeared entirely into a hole, five feet deep. They peered over the edge to see their nanny standing on top of an old wooden chest.

'Could you help me pull this up, Boris?' asked Nanny Piggins. 'It's very heavy – partly because it's heavy and partly because I'm standing on it.'

Boris reached into the hole and easily pulled up both his sister and the chest. There was a huge old-fashioned lock on the front of it.

'You'll never get that open,' said Derrick.

'Hmm, I think I will,' said Nanny Piggins. 'After all, they didn't have hairpins back in the olden days so they wouldn't have thought to make this lock hairpin proof.'

Nanny Piggins plucked a hairpin from her hair (that she wore specifically for breaking into locks, which she found herself having to do with surprising regularity), and in a matter of seconds the lock sprang open. 'Gotcha!' exclaimed Nanny Piggins with delight.

'Not so fast!' barked a voice from behind them.

They all spun around to see Mr Dulsford, a formidable looking man in his late seventies. Formidable because he had an enormous amount of wrinkles on his face and also because he was wearing a tweed jacket and tie even though it was quite a hot day. (It is odd how we can be intimidated by well-dressed people.)

'You can't stop me from opening this chest,' declared Nanny Piggins. 'Yes, it is on your property. And yes, we are trespassing. And yes, technically, in the eyes of the law, anything on your property is yours. But I found it. It's my treasure map so I say it's mine!'

'Of course it's yours!' said Mr Dulsford, a big smile breaking across his face. 'That's why I've been throwing treasure maps out of my car window all these years.'

'What?!' exclaimed the children.

'Because you're the great-great-great grandson of a pirate with a very specific will?' guessed Nanny Piggins.

'No, because when I was a young man I explored the world – the Arctic, the Antarctic, the Amazon . . .' said Mr Dulsford.

'Really?' asked Nanny Piggins. 'Did you meet my friend Barry? He's a boa constrictor from Brazil. A tremendous fellow. He can open a baked-bean tin just by squeezing it. Not that anyone in their right mind would want to open a tin of beans, but Barry was just the chap to have around if you didn't have a can opener.'

'Can't say that I did,' said Mr Dulsford.

'That's a shame,' said Nanny Piggins. 'Anyway, you were explaining this ridiculous charade?'

'Yes, well, I'm old and don't get out much now. So I wanted to meet some fellow adventurers,' said Mr Dulsford, getting a wistful look on his face. 'People who know how to face down fear, overcome obstacles and break the pole-vaulting world record to get over a 31 foot solid wall.'

'That is us,' conceded Nanny Piggins.

'So you put the treasure here and you left the map by the side of the road?' asked Michael.

'Yes, I've been doing it for years,' explained Mr Dulsford, 'but you are the first people to make it this far. Usually people get stopped by the wall, or they get savaged by the dogs while they're waist deep in quicksand. Perhaps I need to add some more obstacles.'

'So you're a crazy old man with more money than sense?' summarised Nanny Piggins. 'Does that mean we can keep this treasure?'

'Of course, it's all yours!' said Mr Dulsford happily.

Not needing any further invitation, Nanny Piggins flipped open the lid to reveal a huge pile of gold coins.

'Hurray!' yelled Nanny Piggins triumphantly, before grabbing a handful of coins and tossing them in her mouth.

The others were shocked for a second until Nanny Piggins spat them back out. 'Pah! Pah!' spat Nanny Piggins. 'They're made of real solid gold!!!'

'Of course,' said Mr Dulsford. 'What were you expecting?'

'Chocolate coins,' said Nanny Piggins. 'You know, the type you get in Christmas stockings.'

'Well, I naturally assumed –' began Mr Dulsford.

'Who'd want a pile of silly old gold?' interrupted Nanny Piggins. 'If I wanted to dig for gold I'd be a gold miner. When I go digging for treasure I expect to dig up something good.'

'I'm sorry, I don't have any chocolate,' said Mr Dulsford, taken aback.

'No chocolate!' exclaimed Nanny Piggins. 'No wonder you're so eccentric. How about a nice chocolate cake? I'd settle for that.'

'I don't think I have any cake in the house,' said Mr Dulsford.

'How can you be a rich eccentric old man and not have chocolate or chocolate cake in your house?' asked Nanny Piggins. 'What's the point of having all that money if you don't spend at least some of it, preferably most of it, on cake?!'

'Er . . .' began Mr Dulsford. He had never thought about it this way.

'Never mind,' said Nanny Piggins. 'I can see I'll just have to take you in hand. Because let me tell you, there are a lot better and less elaborate ways to make friends than forging pirate maps and setting up impossibly dangerous obstacles in your own garden.'

'There are?' asked Mr Dulsford. While he was a great adventurer, he was socially clueless.

'Oh yes,' said Nanny Piggins, 'and baking chocolate cake is one of them. Come along, let's leave this rubbish here. I'll take you back to the house and show you how to make some real priceless treasure.'

And so, in one afternoon, Nanny Piggins transformed Mr Dulsford's life with cake.

'Are you sure this is going to work?' asked Mr Dulsford as he took his very first piping hot chocolate cake out of the oven.

'Trust me, no-one with a cake that smells this good is going to be lonely for long,' said Nanny Piggins.

And at that exact moment, to prove her right, the doorbell rang.

DING-DONG.

'There, you see,' said Nanny Piggins.

'But surely no-one can smell this cake from right out on the street,' said Derrick.

'Maybe, maybe not,' said Nanny Piggins, 'but even some super sensitive humans have a touch of what we pigs call our sixth sense – the ability to sense the presence of cake.'

Mr Dulsford clicked on the monitor displaying a security camera feed. It showed a mousy woman waiting by the front gate.

'But it's only the woman who comes around collecting clothes for charity,' said Mr Dulsford.

'Invite her in for a slice of cake,' urged Nanny Piggins. 'If you do, I guarantee she'll be back again next week, perhaps even tomorrow.'

And so thanks to Nanny Piggins, the richest (and most eccentric) man in Dulsford made a new friend. (Something that is always a lot harder than it sounds.) Word quickly spread about his chocolate cake-making ability and soon all the widows and spinsters of Dulsford were finding excuses to pop by and visit him.

Mr Dulsford was so grateful he tried to make a large donation to Nanny Piggins' mayoral campaign. But naturally she refused him.

'I don't need money,' said Nanny Piggins. 'When you are as glamorous and talented as I am, there are very few things that money can buy.'

'But there must be some way I can help,' protested Mr Dulsford.

'I'll tell you what,' said Nanny Piggins. 'You can give me something of real value.'

'What's that?' asked Mr Dulsford.

'On election day, you can bake me a cake to celebrate my election victory,' declared Nanny Piggins.

'It would be my honour,' said Mr Dulsford.

'But Nanny Piggins,' said Samantha. 'What if you lose?'

'Well then, you had better make me two cakes,' said Nanny Piggins, 'because I'll need cheering up.'

'Deal,' said Mr Dulsford.

# CHAPTER 10

*Nanny Piggins and the Election Day*

It was Election Day, so the children were surprised when they came down to breakfast to discover that their nanny was not there.

'Where's Nanny Piggins?' asked Derrick suspiciously.

Their father was jauntily whistling off-tune as he read the paper and munched on his high-fibre breakfast cereal.

'I don't know,' said Mr Green. He disliked being

directly addressed by his children. It always took him by surprise. He had liked it much better when they were younger and could not talk, walk, or follow him when he left the house.

'You haven't had her arrested, have you?' asked Samantha suspiciously.

'Or kidnapped?' asked Michael.

'Or deported?' asked Derrick.

'Of course not,' said Mr Green. 'I'm a busy man. This afternoon I'm going to be elected Mayor of Dulsford. It would be beneath my dignity to be involved in the abduction of a pig.'

'You mean you hadn't thought of it before now,' guessed Michael shrewdly.

At that moment Mr Green was saved from further cross-examination by the ring of the telephone. Michael went to answer it and soon hurried back.

'That was Nanny Piggins,' said Michael. 'She's upstairs in her bedroom.'

'Then how did she ring us?' asked Samantha.

'She used two hankies tied to chopsticks to wave a semaphore message to Mrs Simpson next door,' explained Michael, 'and told her to phone us.'

'What does Nanny Piggins want?' asked Derrick.

'She wants us to bring some breakfast up to her,' explained Michael.

'Is she all right?' asked Samantha.

'I think so,' said Michael. 'She asked for two dozen chocolate croissants, a mud cake, a litre of chocolate milk and as many doughnuts as we could carry. So she sounds like she hasn't lost her appetite.'

A few minutes later the children lugged the considerable breakfast up the stairs and along the corridor to Nanny Piggins' room. Samantha knocked on the door.

'Come in,' called Nanny Piggins.

Samantha pushed open the door and they all peered in. They were disconcerted to discover their nanny still lying in bed. Oddly, she was fully dressed in a powder blue twin-set with pearls. But she was in bed under the covers nonetheless.

'Is everything all right?' asked Derrick.

'I think so,' said Nanny Piggins.

'Why are you still in bed?' asked Michael.

'It has only just occurred to me that, come this evening, I may very well be Mayor of Dulsford,' said Nanny Piggins.

'But you've been working towards that for months,' said Michael.

'I know,' agreed Nanny Piggins, 'but I do a great number of things heedless of the consequences. I'm forever jumping off buildings, blasting out of cannons and diving into crocodile infested waters, never thinking about what I'm going to do next until I'm hurtling towards the bitumen or a croco- dile's open jaws. So I have only just realised that I may soon be responsible for the running of this whole town.'

'But you take charge of things all the time,' said Derrick.

'Yes, but that's different,' agued Nanny Piggins. 'I've never been *given* responsibility before, I've only ever taken it or had it thrust upon me.'

'What worries you about that?' asked Samantha.

'This could be the thin edge of the wedge,' said Nanny Piggins. 'First I'm elected mayor. Then what? Am I going to have to start behaving responsibly in public? Will I have to iron my clothes? Will I have to stop yelling at the people in the post office?'

'I don't think anyone will expect you to do that,' Derrick assured her.

'I think people like that you do those things,' said Michael.

'Being a politician isn't that big a deal,' Samantha assured her. 'If you don't like it you can always cause some sort of chocolate-related scandal and force yourself to resign.'

'That's a good idea,' said Nanny Piggins, perking up. 'I could eat all the government's chocolate reserves.'

'I know the government has oil and gold reserves, but I don't think they have chocolate reserves,' said Derrick.

'Piffle,' said Nanny Piggins. 'Of course they have chocolate reserves. Why do you think so many politicians are overweight?'

'Because they work long hours and don't exercise?' suggested Samantha.

'Work?!' scoffed Nanny Piggins. 'What they do isn't work. All they do is argue with each other, go to supermarket openings and shake people's hands. And they only do that for a few hours a week. The rest of the week they spend down in a deep bunker underneath the town hall, guzzling chocolate bars.'

'How do you know?' asked Michael.

'It only makes sense,' said Nanny Piggins. 'If you had ultimate authority over everyone and could do whatever you liked, what would you do all day long?'

Michael thought about it. 'Do they have video games as well as chocolate in the underground bunker?' he asked.

'Definitely,' said Nanny Piggins. 'They've probably got pinball machines too.'

'Then that's what they're doing,' agreed Michael.

'So is that what you want to do?' asked Samantha. 'You don't have to be mayor. You could always run away.'

'Run away!' cried Nanny Piggins, throwing back the covers and leaping out of bed. 'I never run away. I'm a Piggins!'

'Bramwell is a Piggins,' pointed out Derrick, 'and he runs away all the time.'

'I forgot about him,' admitted Nanny Piggins. 'If he didn't look exactly like us and have the same last name I'd find it very hard to believe he was a Piggins at all. But the female Pigginses never run away.'

'You ran away from the circus,' Michael pointed out.

'And you often run away from the Police Sergeant and the Truancy Officer, and Nanny Anne when she starts giving you cooking tips,' added Samantha.

'Okay, on a few select occasions I run away for tactical reasons,' agreed Nanny Piggins, 'but never out of cowardice. I only ever run away out of bravery because I know I can run faster than the Police Sergeant, or that if I put up with the Ringmaster a moment longer I shall be arrested for throwing him in a river.'

'That's true,' agreed Derrick. Samantha and Michael nodded as well.

'So there is no way I am going to let my natural revulsion to responsibility, organised government or men wearing grey suits stop me from standing for this election today, trouncing my opponents and taking over Dulsford,' declared Nanny Piggins.

'You mean running Dulsford responsibly on behalf of the people who elect you,' suggested Samantha.

'I've never promised I was going to do that,' said Nanny Piggins. 'That would be ridiculous. Come along, we need to fetch Boris and get down to the polling station so I can cast a vote for myself.'

It took some time to get ready to go out because Nanny Piggins insisted that everyone look very glamorous in case the paparazzi – or, more realistically, the photographer from the local paper – was there to take their pictures. Which meant they all had to dress up like movie stars with big sunglasses, ostentatious jewellery, unseasonably skimpy clothes and pouty smiles. This was tremendous fun and involved changing in and out of many outfits, and arguing over who was going to wear which panama hat.

Eventually they made it down to the school where the polling station had been set up.

'Not you,' said Headmaster Pimplestock ungraciously as Nanny Piggins approached the school. He was standing outside the gate, handing out 'how to vote' cards for Mayor Bloomsbridge.

'What are you doing here?' demanded Nanny Piggins.

'It's my school,' declared Headmaster Pimplestock. 'I have every right to be here.'

'I suppose,' said Nanny Piggins begrudgingly, 'but why are you handing out those cards?'

'I want to make sure you don't win,' said Headmaster Pimplestock.

'What?!' exclaimed Nanny Piggins. 'After everything I've done for you!'

'What do you mean?' wailed Headmaster Pimplestock. 'I've lost count of the number of times you've stomped on my foot, bitten my shin or leapt over my desk and attacked me.'

'If you knew how many times I'd wanted to do it and restrained myself you'd be more grateful,' said Nanny Piggins.

'Goodness knows what damage you'd do if you became mayor,' said Headmaster Pimplestock.

'The unemployment rate among headmasters

would increase, that's for sure,' muttered Nanny Piggins.

'Mayor Bloomsbridge has a proper respect for education,' accused Headmaster Pimplestock.

'Pish!' said Nanny Piggins. 'You just mean he came to visit you and brought you a packet of choc-olate biscuits.'

Headmaster Pimplestock gasped. 'How do you know?'

'I can smell them on your breath,' said Nanny Piggins, sniffing the headmaster. 'Choc-mint biscuits . . .' She sniffed again. 'A fortnight ago you ate an entire packet but one. I can only assume you let the mayor eat one biscuit himself.'

'Are you accusing me of accepting a bribe?' asked Headmaster Pimplestock.

'I wasn't planning to,' said Nanny Piggins. 'I would never begrudge anybody a chocolate biscuit, especially not a free one. But if you want to admit that you took a bribe and are, therefore, shockingly immoral, I'm prepared to accept that.'

'I did no such thing,' fibbed Headmaster Pimplestock.

'You really need to train your eyelid to stop twitching whenever you tell a great big fib,' said Boris.

'You'll never win at poker when your facial muscles are more honest than you are,' agreed Nanny Piggins. 'Now get out of my way, I haven't got time to argue with you. I have come to vote.'

'Just make sure you don't damage any school property,' Headmaster Pimplestock called after them.

'I wasn't intending to damage any school property,' Nanny Piggins called back, 'but if you keep irritating me, I will take time out of my schedule to toilet paper your car later.'

'Come on, Nanny Piggins, he's not worth it,' said Derrick, taking his nanny by the arm and leading her down the path to the school hall.

Unfortunately, when they got there, there were even further delays because the school's P&C association was holding a bake sale. A trestle table full of cakes, biscuits and tarts was laid out alongside the queue of people waiting to vote.

As soon as Nanny Piggins saw it, she gasped with delight. 'Is this for me?' she gushed. 'You shouldn't have! But I'm glad you did.'

'Nanny Piggins, the cakes are for sale,' explained Samantha hurriedly. 'They are to raise money for the school.'

But it was too late. Trying to explain something

to Nanny Piggins when she had cake in her sights was like trying to explain something to a lion when it had a side of wildebeest in its mouth.

Nanny Piggins ran over to the table, leapt onto the cakes and started devouring them. It actually held up the voting process for some time because all the people waiting to vote stopped to watch Nanny Piggins guzzle the entire table load of food.

Now, you might think that this public display of gluttony would disgust the assembled crowd. But on the contrary, Nanny Piggins was so athletic and graceful in the way she shovelled food into her mouth it was a spectacular sight to behold. A bit like watching a ballet if ballet dancers ever did a ballet about eating food. And Nanny Piggins was very generous. When she came across a particularly delicious cake or biscuit she would cry out with delight, 'Oh my goodness, this is divine, you must all try some.' Then she would rush up to the queue of people and jam chunks of cake into their mouths. Upon which they would all start moaning with delight and agreeing that it was delicious.

'Nanny Piggins, what are you doing?' asked Derrick between mouthfuls of treacle tart that his nanny was hand-feeding him. 'Those cakes aren't free, you are going to have to pay for them.'

'You must have eaten three or four hundred dollars' worth of cake,' worried Samantha.

'It will be worth every penny,' said Nanny Piggins, licking shredded coconut from her snout. 'I never knew the democratic process involved cake! Otherwise I would have taken up politics much earlier.'

'Do you have three or four hundred dollars?' asked Michael.

'No,' admitted Nanny Piggins, 'but I'll write the school an IOU and then pay them back when I become mayor. Being mayor is an important job so I'm sure it comes with a cake allowance.'

'I don't think it does,' said Derrick.

'Then the very first thing I'll do when I'm elected is give everyone in the town a cake allowance!' declared Nanny Piggins.

'Hooray!' cried everyone in the queue.

Nanny Piggins rejoined the line and slowly snaked her way to the front where she could get her name marked off the electoral roll and receive her ballot paper.

'Name?' said the electoral worker at the front of the queue.

'My name is Sarah Matahari Lorelei Piggins,' declared Nanny Piggins, 'and I am the world's greatest flying pig.'

'Piggins,' said the electoral worker. 'How do you spell that? With a P?'

'How else would you spell Piggins?' asked Michael.

'Michael,' chided Nanny Piggins, 'you must never be rude to someone who doesn't know how to spell. You should be envious that their head isn't filled with so much twaddle and claptrap.'

'You're not here,' said the electoral worker.

'Yes I am,' said Nanny Piggins. 'I'm standing right in front of you.'

'No, you're not on the electoral roll,' said the electoral worker. 'There are no Pigginses.'

'That is an outrage!' denounced Nanny Piggins. 'How dare you exclude me.'

'Nanny Piggins,' said Samantha, an unpleasant idea beginning to dawn. 'You did register to vote, didn't you?'

'Whatgister to do what-what?' asked Nanny Piggins.

'Register to vote,' said Samantha. 'If you want to vote, you have to fill in a form and register yourself on the electoral roll.'

'You mean I have to voluntarily put myself on a government list?' asked Nanny Piggins.

'Yes,' said the children.

'As if I would ever do that!' exclaimed Nanny Piggins. 'When the government comes looking for me, I'm hardly going to make it easy for them by registering myself and my address on a list.'

'All citizens have to,' said Derrick.

'Ah, well there you go,' said Nanny Piggins, 'that's why I never did it. Because I'm not a citizen either.'

'You're not a citizen?!' exclaimed Derrick.

'Of course not,' said Nanny Piggins. 'I'm a pig. We like to live like gypsies, independent from society's structures.'

'But what on earth made you think you could run for mayor if you're not even a citizen?' wailed Samantha.

'What are you saying?' asked Nanny Piggins. 'I can't run for mayor just because the government has no record of my existence? Well, that's very nitpicky of them. Surely they wouldn't be so petty.'

'I think people in government like being petty,' said Boris. 'They're good at it.'

'It'll be fine,' said Nanny Piggins. 'All of you will just have to make sure you vote for me twice.'

The children looked at each other.

'Er . . .' said Derrick, not knowing how he was going to explain what he had to explain without getting yelled at. 'No-one can vote twice. That's how the system works. Everyone gets one vote.'

'What? Even beautiful people on television and people who make chocolate for a living?!' asked Nanny Piggins.

'Yes,' said Samantha.

'Now that doesn't seem fair,' argued Nanny Piggins. 'That someone as accomplished and important as Hans the baker should only get one vote, just the same as someone as useless and insignificant as Headmaster Pimplestock.'

'Also,' said Derrick bravely, 'we can't vote because we are children. You have to be over 18 to vote.'

'No!' gasped Nanny Piggins. 'But how do they know how old you are? It's rude to ask a lady's age!'

'They're the government,' said Michael. 'They just know.'

'This is precisely why I never register anything with them,' said Nanny Piggins. 'So you're saying none of us can vote?'

'Actually,' said Boris, looking a little sheepish, 'I can.'

'But you're Russian,' said Nanny Piggins.

'Technically I'm a duel citizen,' said Boris. 'I studied the electoral process at law school and it sounded like a lot of fun so I took up citizenship so I could join in.'

'Why didn't you tell me?' asked Nanny Piggins.

'The day I did it was the day your chocolate sponge cake went flat in the oven,' explained Boris.

Nanny Piggins let out one loud sob before she managed to contain her emotions. 'That was a dark day,' she whispered.

'I know,' said Boris. 'You were devastated. I didn't like to bother you with my national allegiances.'

'Well hurry up and vote for me, because Mr Green is definitely going to vote for Mr Green and Mayor Bloomsbridge is definitely going to vote for Mayor Bloomsbridge so we need you to counteract their votes,' said Nanny Piggins.

'All right,' said Boris. 'I brought along a honey sandwich so I could have a little picnic in the booth while I was voting.'

'Good thinking,' said Nanny Piggins. 'It would be awful if you got low blood sugar, your vision went blurry and you accidentally voted for Mr Green.'

So Boris disappeared into the little cardboard booth with his ballot paper and studiously filled it out.

'It's a shame we ate all the cake at the cake stall,' said Nanny Piggins as they stood waiting for him to finish. 'I'm feeling a little peckish.'

When five minutes stretched into ten minutes and then fifteen, Nanny Piggins began to get restless.

'I don't want to pressure my brother,' said Nanny Piggins, 'but he does seem to be taking an inordinately long time to vote. There are only three names on the ballot. Even allowing for a little break to eat his honey sandwich, I don't see what could be taking him so long.'

'Perhaps he's fallen into one of his super-deep hibernation sleeps?' guessed Samantha.

'I doubt it,' said Nanny Piggins. 'It's not cold enough. Besides, he got a full fifteen hours of sleep last night so he should be perky enough.'

'Do you want me to go and see if he's all right?' asked Michael.

'You're not meant to interfere with someone while they're voting,' said Derrick.

'I'll whisper so that I don't distract him,' said Michael.

So Michael walked over to Boris and squeezed between his legs. (Boris was so big and the voting booth was so small, he almost entirely filled it up. The only way for Michael to talk to Boris was to get down on his hands and knees, crawl between his legs, then pull himself up on the voting shelf where they could have a conversation.)

Michael disappeared from view for several seconds before reappearing, by crawling back out through Boris' legs.

'What's going on?' asked Nanny Piggins.

'He's stuck,' explained Michael. 'The booth is so small that he has wedged himself in and now he can't get out. And he's quite upset because he thinks the booth is shrinking because he can't see how else it could have possibly happened.'

'He does realise that he is a great big ten-foot-tall Kodiak bear and that the voting booth is just made of cardboard?' asked Nanny Piggins.

'I did point that out,' said Michael, 'but he says he doesn't want to damage anything in case they won't invite him back to vote next time.'

'I'll get him out of there,' said Nanny Piggins with a steely glint in her eye.

She walked over and stood directly behind her brother before shrieking, 'Aaaaaaagggggghhhhhhh!!!!! Mouse!!!'

Boris exited the voting booth directly upwards because he leapt so high in the air. Luckily Nanny Piggins then stepped out of the way, otherwise he would have landed on her when he came down with an enormous thud.

'Where?!' panicked Boris. 'Oooh, I do so hate mice. Then are so mean and bitey. And they eat my honey sandwiches.'

'It's all right. It's gone now,' said Nanny Piggins as she gave her brother a comforting hug. 'So now, all we have to do is wait for the polls to close and the results to be announced. I believe it is customary to wait in a public place where there are plenty of refreshments available, preferably cakey ones.'

'Did you have somewhere in mind?' asked Derrick.

'I thought perhaps Hans' Bakery,' said Nanny Piggins.

'Ooooh, can I have a slice of cake?' asked Boris.

'We'll have many, many slices of cake,' declared Nanny Piggins. 'After all, the polls don't close for another five hours, then it will take them at least ten minutes to see that I'm the clear winner. And I can eat a lot of cake in five hours and ten minutes.'

'And you don't think it will affect your ability to be mayor, the fact that you aren't registered to vote or even a citizen of this country?' asked Michael as they turned to leave.

'Not at all,' said Nanny Piggins. 'I'm sure nobody

can be bothered checking such tedious things, so how would they ever find out?'

Unfortunately at that very moment Nanny Piggins came face-to-face with her answer, because Mr Green was standing right behind them, and from the joyous expression on his face he looked as though he had just got the biggest tax return of his life.

'You aren't a registered citizen?!' he exclaimed.

Nanny Piggins did momentarily consider lying (which I know is wicked of her, but it really is Mr Green's fault for bringing out the worst in her). 'Technically, no,' she admitted.

'You aren't going to do anything about it, are you, Father?' asked Michael naively. He knew the answer before his father even spoke, because Mr Green's eyes were bugging out of his head from excitement.

'You aren't a registered citizen!' he declared again.

'Yes, we've covered that,' said Nanny Piggins with a sigh. 'You really are the most tedious person to hold a conversation with.'

'Who do I tell first?' asked Mr Green. Not that he was talking to anyone else, he was more babbling to himself with hysterical glee. 'The newspapers?

The television reporters? The electoral authorities? Oooh, I know! I'll hold a press conference.'

'Please, Father,' pleaded Samantha. 'Don't do that. Nanny Piggins would make a wonderful mayor. Much better than you. On some level you must know that.'

'I know no such thing,' said Mr Green. 'She is a pig. At least I'm a human.'

'A sorry example of one,' said Nanny Piggins. 'Surely it's better to have the world's greatest flying pig be mayor as opposed to the town's most mediocre tax lawyer.'

But Mr Green was not listening. He rarely did when people less important than him were talking, and he thought most people were less important than him. 'Maybe they'll throw her in jail for electoral fraud and I'll finally be free of the dreadful pig.'

'How dare you speak about my sister in that way!' denounced Boris, starting to get angry (which was most unlike him. He usually went straight to weepy, or wracking sobs).

'Who are you?' asked Mr Green, not recognising Boris as the bear who had taught him tap dancing or had been living in his garden shed. 'On second thoughts, don't tell me. I don't have time for any of you. I'm off to report this pig to the appropriate authorities.'

Mr Green turned on his heel and hurried out of the room. Nanny Piggins sighed as she watched him go.

'Does that mean it's all over?' asked Samantha.

'You're not going to be mayor?' asked Derrick disbelievingly.

They could not accept that this political journey should be brought to an end by such a small hurdle. They had always assumed that their nanny would win, as she did with everything, and become the best and most successful politician since her great-great-great Aunt Winston Piggins had dressed up as a man and led the allies to victory in World War II.

'Children,' said Nanny Piggins. 'If my political career were the only concern here, then yes, I'm afraid this would be it. The end of our journey. But there is something much more serious at stake – Dulsford. The town we live in, our home and our way of life is being threatened by that dreadful man – your father.'

'Yes, we knew who you were talking about,' nodded Derrick.

'And so it is not for me, but the children of Dulsford and the children's children of Dulsford for whom I shall now take action,' declared Nanny Piggins.

'What action?' asked Michael.

'I'm going to kidnap your father,' said Nanny Piggins. 'Boris, find a sack.'

'I already have,' said Boris, holding up a large hessian sack. 'I went and found one as soon as I realised he'd overheard us. If you weren't going to kidnap him, I was.'

'Let's do it together,' said Nanny Piggins. 'It's always nice to do things as a family.'

And so, an hour later, Nanny Piggins, Boris and the children sat happily in Hans' Bakery eating cake and watching the election coverage on TV as they awaited the results.

Mr Green was safely locked in Hans' storage room, which Nanny Piggins reasoned could not be viewed as a hardship. She often dreamed of being locked in Hans' storeroom, surrounded by all that cake.

'The polls have been closed for half an hour and according to electoral officials we should soon have a result,' announced the reporter. 'It looks like there is going to be a clear winner.'

'That's you!' said Michael, squeezing his nanny's hand affectionately.

Boris just burst into tears, which was the traditional Russian response to all good news, and all bad news as well.

'We cross now to our reporter at the tally room,' said the anchorman.

'There has been a landslide result,' said the reporter excitedly. '17,861 votes were cast in Dulsford: 2084 for the incumbent mayor. Zero for Lysander Green…'

'How can Father have got no votes at all?' asked Samantha.

'Who would vote for him?' asked Derrick.

'And he didn't get a chance to vote for himself before we kidnapped him,' added Michael.

'So the clear winner, with 15,777 votes, is Sarah Matahari Lorelei Piggins, World's Greatest Flying Pig!' announced the reporter.

A huge cheer went up in the tally room behind the reporter and in the bakery where Nanny Piggins and the children were sitting. Quite a crowd of her supporters had gathered to be with her when she won power. There was the retired Army Colonel who lived round the corner (and was secretly in love with Nanny Piggins), Mrs Lau from across the street, the Police Sergeant, Mrs Hesselstein from the Chocolatorium, Mrs Simpson next door, Stan the truck driver, Rosalind the bearded lady, Melanie the fat lady, Mr Dulsford the eccentric billionaire as well as dozens more friends and neighbours who had all squeezed into the bakery to be there when the result was announced.

'Three cheers for Nanny Piggins!' cried the retired Army Colonel. 'Hip hip –'

'Wait!' yelled Nanny Piggins. Silence fell on the crowd and they all turned to look where Nanny Piggins' outstretched trotter was pointing. On the television screen they could see Mr Green and he looked dishevelled. Journalists and TV cameras were crowded around him. 'He must have escaped!'

'Nanny Piggins cannot be mayor because she is not a registered voter or even a citizen of this country,' cried Mr Green. 'She doesn't exist. She's nothing but a common pink farm pig!'

'Can you prove it?' cried a journalist.

'No, because there is no evidence,' cried Mr Green. 'She has no paperwork. And you can't be mayor if you don't exist.'

A dreadful silence fell in the bakery.

'What does this mean?' asked Derrick.

'It means your father is going to get a nasty surprise in his high-fibre breakfast cereal tomorrow morning,' said Nanny Piggins.

'But what does this mean for the election results?' asked Samantha.

'I don't know,' admitted Nanny Piggins.

They all turned back to look at the television. An electoral official was now addressing the media scrum.

'In cases where the elected mayor cannot accept the appointment . . .' said the official loudly over the excited babble of the crowd.

'What happens?' cried a journalist. 'Does the incumbent mayor win by default?'

Everyone groaned at the prospect.

'No,' said the official firmly. 'If the elected mayor cannot accept the appointment, the second person on his, or in this case her, ticket then becomes mayor.'

Everyone in the bakery turned to look at Nanny Piggins.

'Who was second on your ticket?' asked Derrick.

'I didn't even know you had a second person on your ticket,' said Michael.

Nanny Piggins had gone white with shock. 'Well, I filled out the form such a long time ago,' said Nanny Piggins, 'I didn't know who to put. I didn't think it would matter. So I just put . . . Boris.'

Everyone turned to look at Boris.

'What,' said Boris, looking up from his honey cake. 'What's going on? Sorry I wasn't following the conversation. I was enjoying my honey cake.'

'Boris,' said Samantha gently, 'you are the newly elected Mayor of Dulsford.'

And for once Boris did not react to a great surprise by bursting into tears. He could not because he had fainted flat on the floor. So he, as well as a great many other people at the party, had to eat an enormous amount of cake to overcome the shock before he could go down to the Town Hall to make his acceptance speech.

'People of Dulsford,' began Boris. 'I want to assure you that as your newly elected mayor I will not just represent the people who voted for me . . .'

'That's good,' said Derrick, 'because no-one voted for him.'

'But the people who didn't vote for me as well,' said Boris.

There was smattering of half-hearted clapping from the crowd.

Boris bent down to whisper to Michael. 'They don't seem to like me very much.'

'Say something cheerful,' suggested Michael.

Boris stood up straight and addressed the crowd again. 'Under my leadership,' said Boris, 'there will be honey sandwiches and nap time for all!'

This declaration got a much bigger round of applause.

'Leaf blowers will be banned from use before noon so that everyone can sleep in,' announced Boris. 'Bus seats will be made wider to accommodate the bigger boned; fairy floss will be handed out free at the library during story time and I will personally give yoga lessons in the park every day!'

Now there was a huge cheer from the crowd and Boris happily waved at the people.

'You know,' said Nanny Piggins, 'I get the sneaking suspicion that Boris is going to make a very good politician.'

'You aren't disappointed to lose?' asked Michael.

'Not at all,' said Nanny Piggins. 'It was the best possible result for me. I achieved all my goals. I trounced your father and the incumbent mayor. And now, I don't actually have to do any of the work, so I can spend more time with you three.' She hugged the children affectionately. 'It's a win-win-win-win scenario.'

# The Nanny Piggins Guide
# to Conquering Christmas

by R. A. Spratt

will be in all pig-approved bookshops
in November 2013

# Loved the book?

There's so much more
stuff to check out online

AUSTRALIAN READERS:

randomhouse.com.au/kids

NEW ZEALAND READERS:

randomhouse.co.nz/kids